Painting Tacoma

A Novel

I0659165

by

Michael J. Vaughn

John P. Rutledge, Editor

FIRST EDITION

2004

ISBN 1-929429-92-4

THIS LITERARY WORK WAS CREATED IN THE UNITED STATES OF AMERICA, IS COPYRIGHT © 2003 BY MICHAEL J. VAUGHN (DEAD END STREET, LLC, EXCLUSIVE LICENSEE) AND IS REGISTERED WITH THE UNITED STATES COPYRIGHT OFFICE. ALL RIGHTS RESERVED. ALL COVER ART WAS CREATED BY KNOLL GILBERT AND IS COPYRIGHT © 2003 BY DEAD END STREET, LLC. THIS WORK HAS BEEN FORMATTED BY DEAD END STREET® WITH THE AUTHOR'S EXPRESS PERMISSION.

THIS LITERARY WORK IS LARGELY FICTION. NO SIMILARITY TO ACTUAL PERSONS, LIVING OR DEAD, IS INTENDED OR SHOULD BE INFERRED, UNLESS SUCH PERSON(S) IS/ARE EXPRESSLY IDENTIFIED BY NAME. NO ONE IS INTENTIONALLY DEFAMED OR EXPLOITED IN THIS WORK IN VIOLATION OF ANY RIGHT OF PUBLICITY LAW. LIKEWISE, NO INTELLECTUAL PROPERTY RIGHT OF ANY PARTY WAS INTENTIONALY VIOLATED IN THIS WORK. THE AUTHOR AND PUBLISHER ARE WILLING TO CONSIDER AMENDING THIS TEXT TO ERADICATE ANY UNLAWFUL LANGUAGE, DESCRIPTION OR CONTENT.

ALL RIGHTS RESERVED. NO PART OF THIS LITERARY WORK (AND/OR ANY ACCOMPANYING ARTWORK) MAY BE REPRODUCED IN ANY MANNER WITHOUT THE EXPRESS, WRITTEN CONSENT OF DEAD END STREET, LLC (EXCEPT IN THE CASE OF BRIEF QUOTATIONS EMBODIED IN CRITICAL ARTICLES AND REVIEWS). FOR INFORMATION OR CONSENT, PLEASE CONTACT:

JOHN P. RUTLEDGE, PRESIDENT & GENERAL COUNSEL
DEAD END STREET, LLC
813 THIRD STREET
HOQUIAM, WA 98550
jrutledge@deadendstreet.com

DEAD END STREET® is a registered service mark of Dead End Street, LLC.

For my favorite clients – Calder Lowe and Nina Koepcke –
and for the Russian princess.

Gray

Reverend Fisher stood in the shower, feeling uninspired. His soaping process was composed of carefully mapped-out quadrants – left leg, right leg, genitals, etc. – and he had lost his place. He inspected his graying chest hair for suds — then felt a drip along his sideburns.

Well, he thought. *Now we're getting somewhere.* Rather than trying to figure out where he was in the shampooing process, he grabbed his Herbal Essence and started over.

I am terribly distracted, he thought. If it weren't for all the goshdarn mumbo-jumbo of his radio ministry: pledge drives, FCC paperwork, the paucity of late-night filler (how he hated those Southern redneck preachers!) Not to mention his new intern, Daisy McPhillips, the geometry of whose derriere had him grappling with temptation every time she walked away from his desk, or – God help us! – bent over to pick up a file.

But today was Sunday, and the Reverend felt an obligation to deliver joy unto his flock, whether he felt it or not. He dipped his head under the shower stream and came back with his answer. Grandma's song! "Put On A Happy Face." He whistled the tune and felt immediately better.

Emma Fisher stood in the next room, ironing her husband's shirt, fending off a squadron of anxieties. Late last night, she happened on her daughter Wendy in the hallway, and saw in the girl's face a flush of warmth — a flush, let's face it, of a sexual nature. Maybe not actual activity, but Emma remembered what nineteen was like, all those hormones rambling around like free-range chickens.

And then there was her husband, who had suddenly taken to

manhandling her rear end. Last night they had even done it — how did the kids put it? Puppy-style? Marcus grew terribly excited, and at one point even spanked her! Just thinking of it set her skin tingling. But still, it was a change, and Emma Fisher did not respond well to change.

And now the whistling. She knew what that song meant. It meant that he, too, was distracted, and trying to corral some phony enthusiasm for today's sermon. He was a damn fine whistler, though. He had played cornet in high school, and liked to throw in trills and countermelodies as he whistled along with the radio. She found herself humming along, though she could never remember the title. Something about putting on your makeup.

After seeing her husband off, Emma headed to the Mavrovitis Bakery. She supposed she could get away with some of those dry cookies from Safeway, but being the pastor's wife, she felt obligated to do better. The Women's League was welcoming new members, and she thought the occasion called for George's burnt almond cake — a concoction that had the same effect on Emma as last night's slap on the butt.

Phony enthusiasm was a large part of George's occupation, too — but not when it came to Emma Fisher. Mrs. Fisher knew the value of a quality cake, and didn't give in to those low-budget sirens at the Ellensburg Safeway. She was also not bad to look at – something about that thick black hair, the way it set off her blue eyes. George fetched Mrs. Fisher's cake – iced with a cursive *Congratulations!* – and held it up over the counter.

"So lovely!" said Emma, beaming. "I do have to rush off, though. Could you put this on my tab?"

"For the Reverend's wife, always." He slid the pink box into Mrs. Fisher's hands and watched her walk off, holding the door open with her hip as she navigated around the goat bells. *Those hips*, thought George. *How did I not notice those before?* She was humming a tune, too. "Sunny Side of the Street," or something like that.

It wasn't till an hour later, working on butterscotch cupcakes for Billy Johanssen's birthday, that the song snuck its way back in. George didn't even realize he was whistling until Joseph Standing Bear burst through the door.

"What the hell are you so happy about?"

"Oh, hi Bear. Whatcha up to?"

"Got tomorrow off work. MLK Day. Goin' to Cle Elum Lake for some fishin'"

"Kinda cold there, ain't it?"

"Yeah, sure," said Bear. "But the tribe's got a real nice cabin. One o' them big freestanding fireplaces to warm your tootsies. If I don't get any bites, I'll make an early day of it."

"Hell. Why fish at all?"

"Justification, my friend."

"Yeah," said George, laughing. He finished a frill and set down his icing tube. "Always wondered, Bear. Do the guys in the tribe resent all those years you spent at Microsoft?"

"Yeah. They call me an 'Apple Indian.' Red on the outside, white on the inside. But I notice it doesn't come up when they're having problems with their hard drives."

"Hah!" said George. "That's good. Whatcha up for?"

"How's about two peanut butter cookies and a Big Mama coffee?"

"Gotcha." He flipped a cup under the coffeemaker.

It was a great day for driving, so clear and bright it hurt Bear's eyes. He also had to pee. He pulled off at the Teanaway rest stop, which was, strangely enough, one of his favorite spots on Earth. Back when he worked in Redmond, it meant he was almost home, and on a day like this the view was incredible. Teanaway Ridge, Jolly Mountain, Mt. Stuart. He wondered what the tourists thought of this.

He took a brief scan and strode to the bathroom. But Joseph Standing Bear suffered from a "shy bladder," and even the privacy of a stall wasn't doing the trick. After a minute or two, he tried whistling the song that George was whistling, and that seemed to loosen the pipes.

"Put On A Happy Face" was written by composer Charles Strouse and lyricist Lee Adams in 1960 for the musical *Bye Bye Birdie.* It continued to travel the Wenatchee Mountains that day courtesy of Sam Snowden, a retired Chicagoan taking the RV odyssey with his wife Marnie. Sam heard it while sitting in a stall at the rest stop, then passed it on to Marnie, who carried it into a McDonald's in Renton, just across Lake Washington from Seattle. Behind Marnie in line was Rosie Karmit, an African-American lady on her way to Auburn for a movie date with her aunt. The song's gospel edges reminded Rosie of the Dinah Washington records her mother used to play. She was treating it to a full jazz scat when she pulled up next to Josh Adams at 148th Avenue.

Josh was on the way to the mountains for some snowboarding, and had stopped in Snoqualmie for gas. There, he passed it on to Betsy Herman, an elderly former barmaid working the register.

Twenty minutes later, in stepped Nolan Sorbain, a local kid making his living hanging Sheetrock at the new convalescent home on the main drag. Today was his first day off in three weeks, and he decided to take his over-sized Dodge Ram truck out for a spin. And then there was Shawn Turk.

Shawn stood on the shoulder of the offramp, considering the chess match before him. His drum set was piled on the roadside — the only way he could get to the spare tire at the bottom of his hatchback. It was one of those space-saver models that was stored flat, the tire folded tight to the rim. Therein lay his dilemma. He had been smart enough to buy an inflation canister — but the canister also contained a chemical that professed to repair small punctures. How easy life would be, he reasoned, if he could just mend his tire and be on his way.

Following the instructions, he shook the canister for two minutes then screwed the nozzle onto his valve stem. After twenty breathless seconds, Shawn saw no sign of actual inflation. He stuck his head under the chassis to find bitter-smelling white vapor exiting from a long tear on the inside of his tire.

Shawn fell into the symptoms of utter defeat: limbs dropping, chest falling, life essence leaking out of him as he settled his forehead to the cold roof of his car. A big white truck pulled to the shoulder.

"Hey!" said the driver. "Need some help?"

"Um, yeah!" said Shawn. He walked to the window to find a beefy linebacker type, buzzcut hair, backwards ballcap, Celtic tattoo on his bicep. He seemed friendly.

"You got a cell phone?" asked Shawn. "I think I'm gonna need triple-A."

"Sure." He flipped out his phone and aimed a big thumb at the buttons. "Reception's a little chancy up here, but…"

"'Course, what I really need," said Shawn, "is an air compressor."

The linebacker stopped and let out a grin. He reached behind the seat and pulled out a box that said First-Use Emergency Air Compressor.

"You're shittin' me!" said Shawn.

They hooked the compressor to the truck's cigarette lighter, screwed on the air hose and had the spare two-thirds full when the compressor suddenly stopped.

"Uh-oh," said Shawn. "I think we killed it."

"No sweat," said Linebacker. "Ten-dollar piece of shit from Schuck's. I'm just glad I got a chance to try it out. In any case, that'll get you to a gas station."

Shawn pulled off the air hose and gave the spare a whack with his palm. "Yep. I think that'll do it. Geez, I feel like I should give you something. You totally saved my ass. I got drumsticks. You play drums?"

"Don't worry about it," he said. "It all comes back."

Shawn extended a hand covered in tire-soot. Nolan took it anyway.

"Name's Shawn."

"I'm Nolan."

"Nice bumping into you, man."

"Good luck," said Nolan. He strolled to his truck, threw the dead compressor into the cab and left with a wave.

Shawn took a breath and crouched next to the spare, noting from the sidewall warnings that he would now be driving the freeway into Tacoma at fifty miles per hour. He set to work on the lug nuts as he whistled the tune that Nolan had been whistling. Sunshine? Happy... something? Whatever it was, it made the going a little easier.

Copper

After spending the night in a rest stop, bass drum for a pillow, Shawn rolled into Tacoma, traffic zipping by on either side. He turned into downtown, operating on five-year-old directionals — a high-school field trip to the State History Museum. What he remembered most were the hulking brick buildings, past lives painted on their foreheads: F.S. HARMON MFG. CO., ALBERS BROS. MILLING CO. He passed the inverted copper teacup of Union Station, and then took the A Street exit.

Climbing 9th Street, he found a five-way intersection that felt distinctly New Yorkish. It might have been the Pantages Theater, high white walls with cornices and ornaments, or the stone sculptures marking off a lawn-covered island. But the center of gravity was a triangular building to his right, squeezed to a point by the streets of St. Helens and Broadway. The ground floor hosted a coffeehouse, the tip occupied by a single table, surrounded by glass. That was the spot.

He parked in front of a guitar shop, dashed around the corner and marked one of the terrarium chairs with a windbreaker. He sat there with his coffee and surveyed the new territory: lunching office workers, a beaten-down wanderer with a ragged leather backpack, two old ladies with a Dalmatian. Caffeine had no chance against rest-area sleep, however, and he soon began to doze. After three involuntary head-jerks, he decided to take a hike.

A few blocks uphill he found the Merolino Art Center, overlooking the Pittsburgh-like smokestreams of a paper mill. He turned cattycorner to find a square of limestone brick giving off alternate hues of tan brown and margarine. Nearing the entrance he noted three flags: the Stars and

Stripes, the emerald green of Washington, and the Union Jack. The latter was quickly explained by tall letters spelled out over the entranceway: THE CAMBRIDGE. Shawn fumbled with the intercom till he found a button for the manager.

"Hello, Cambridge Apartments."

The voice was female, friendly but direct.

"Hi, um… I wanted to… Do you have apartments available?"

"Sure. What are you looking for? One-bedroom? Studio?"

I got no friggin' idea, he thought. Hell, two days ago he was livin' at Mom and Dad's.

"Um… a studio's probably fine."

"Good. 'Cause that's all we got." She let out a chirpy laugh. "I'll be down in two minutes."

"Okay. I'm on the hilly side."

"Right. Where the intercom is."

"Oh. Uh, yeah."

Shawn was running a hand over a ceramic-tile gryphon when a remarkably young-looking blonde stuck her head out the doorway.

"Are you the guy?"

"The guy? Yeah, I guess so. Um, Shawn."

She shook his hand. She was thin and wiry, blue eyes set in a small, bird-like face.

"Zasu. And yes, I'm old enough to be the manager. One of these days, I'm going to stop getting that look from people."

"Like Zasu Pitts, the silent film star."

"Hey! Brownie points for the new guy. Come on in. Let's start with 308 – it's my favorite."

They stepped into an elevator, one of those old-fashioned jobs with the accordion-style gate.

"I hate this thing," she said. "Gives me the creeps. I shouldn't even show you 308, you know, because I go up there late at night to write my poetry. But it's really small, so I'm going to knock the rent down from 395 to 380."

The poetry comment had Shawn pretty primed, but he liked it even more when he saw it: hardwood floors, long entranceway, huge old-style bathtub, and two large sash windows framing the downtown skyline. There was just one other thing.

"Can you see the mountain?"

"Sure," she said. "Take a look."

Perhaps this is how you fall in love with a mountain, Shawn thought. *A little bit at a time.* Rainer was peeling a scarf of cloud from her snowy northern shoulder. Shawn painted in the rest of her, hovering just-so over his cityscape.

An hour later he sat on the sidewalk across the street, tucking some paperwork into his windbreaker, when something occurred to him. He found his apartment, just over the Washington flag, and started counting. Five stories, his was the third. Thirteen sets of windows – his was the seventh. The very center.

Salmon

When she heard about his night at the rest area, Zasu let him move in right away.

"But I swear," she added. "If that credit report comes back with multiple bankruptcies, your ass is right back out! And don't tell anyone, 'cause they'd probably fire my butt."

Shawn made impassioned promises, and spent the next hour shuttling his stuff up the stairs. He turned his bass drum sideways for a table and spilled out the contents of his pockets, then headed to the tub for a long soak. He barely had the energy to towel himself off before collapsing on his rolled-out sleeping bag.

Two hours later, he woke to a sunbreak (an indigenous Northwest term), and peered through the half-open blinds to look for his mountain. Alas, she was hiding behind a sandbar of gray, flecked with sunset salmon.

Freshly invigorated, Shawn slapped on his few clean clothes and went for a drive, tooling up Sixth Avenue to find a club district with the usual fringes: vintage clothing, used records, tattoo parlor. When that gave out, he cut left and found a small coffeehouse at the edge of a large shopping center.

When he saw the sign on the door, he almost had to slap himself. Open till midnight — on a Monday, no less! It was true: the streets of Tacoma were paved with gold.

Sitting in the back with a mocha and a *News-Tribune*, he began to notice things. For one, the place was populated exclusively by polite, clean-cut youths (a far cry from the Ellensburg Goths at Café Bovine).

And there was a Bible on his table, next to a napkin reading "Proverbs 3: 3-16." Then there was the music: pretty standard anthem rock, but peppered with words like "lift," "found" and "divine."

Shawn went to Jeff, the friendly-seeming barista, and asked him, as matter-of-factly as possible, "Hey Jeff, is this place sort of a Christian hangout?"

"Oh sure," said Jeff. He was a college kid with one of those chin-liner beards. "Nothing official, but the owner is pretty active at church, plus there's a Christian college up the street. Hey, can you excuse me a sec? Got a song I've been dying to hear."

Jeff headed into the back. A second later, a hip-hop drum track rolled from the speakers, then a professorial voice listing all the synchronicities of Earth's survival (orbits, rotations, distance from the sun) that precluded evolution.

"Isn't that a cool song?" asked Jeff. "I can't believe we teach evolution like it's some kind of fact or something."

"Uh, yeah," said Shawn.

"You know that eruption at Mt. St. Helens a few years ago? They found spots in the resultant mudflow that precisely mimicked natural phenomena that had previously been dated as being billions of years old."

"Wow," said Shawn. He looked at the clock above the smoothie machine. "Oh, man! I was supposed to be at a friend's house fifteen minutes ago. Take it easy, Jeff."

Shawn got into his car, thinking, *I am not about to ruin a perfectly good late-night hangout over a theological debate.* He turned onto 19th and began muttering all the pro-Darwin arguments he might otherwise have used, lacing them with big fat obscenities. He was headed up a small hill when he saw a little white mutt scampering along the sidewalk.

Shawn kept a careful eye on the little dog, which is why he didn't see the big dog until it was too late. Before he could hit the brake, there was a loud thump at his left bumper, and a sickening yelp.

"Shit!"

Shawn regained his steering and pulled into a side street, where a yard full of dogs erupted in a chorus of accusatory barks. He got out and walked back to the main road, half-expecting to find a slushpile of former dog. What he saw was a black Labrador, sitting awkwardly in the turn lane, still and calm. Shawn wasn't really sure what to do, so he knocked at the nearest house to see if they could call animal control.

"Yes, we did that already," said the woman, a middle-aged Hispanic lady. "Did you see who hit him?"

"Yeah," said Shawn. "It was me. Poor guy, he's so dark, he ran out in front of me, and I didn't see him."

"Well, be careful if you go out there. I heard a wounded animal can be kind of snappy."

But someone had beaten him to it. A fortyish blonde woman was slowly approaching the dog, hand held out, speaking in reassuring tones. By the time Shawn got there, she had the dog's head in her lap and was stroking his graying snout.

"Poor thing. Did anybody see who hit him?"

"Yeah," said Shawn. "It was me. He's so dark I didn't even see him." *God*, he thought. *How many more times do I need to make this confession?*

The blonde woman had to leave for work, but she left her card with the Hispanic lady and said she'd like to adopt the dog if he turned out to be a stray. Shawn fetched his car, pulled into the lane behind the dog and switched on his flashers. He draped his windbreaker over the Labrador and knelt beside him, petting his head and making sure he didn't move. He was relieved to see that the line of fluid trailing from the dog's hindquarters was not blood but probably urine.

Shawn sat there another twenty minutes, legs falling asleep, asphalt biting into his thigh. He checked occasionally to make sure the dog was still breathing, and spoke to him in apologetic tones. Two different cops showed up, ten minutes apart, to ask who hit the dog.

Welcome to Tacoma, Shawn. Try not to kill the animals.

When the guy came from the Humane Society, Shawn helped him slip a blanket under the Labrador and load him into the back of the truck. Once they had him settled, two pre-teen girls came around the corner in their pajamas, saying things like "Omigod! Is it Baby?" and, "She isn't dead, is she?" Shawn took the opportunity to head back to the sidewalk. He wrote his new address on an ATM receipt and handed it to the Hispanic lady, asking her to send a note if she heard anything about the dog.

When he turned back around, he was surprised to find that everyone had cleared the scene — except for another cop, who had pulled in behind Shawn's car.

"Sir!" said the cop. "Is this car disabled?"

"No," said Shawn. "I hit a dog, and I was… No, it's fine."

Blue

He woke before dawn and found her silhouetted in orange, holding the sun behind her back like a kid playing keepaway. He knew he wouldn't be going back to sleep, so he headed for the bathroom and discovered another of the apartment's hidden treasures: a toilet-flush that could suck down an Orca.

He decided the immediate thing to do was walk down to the terrarium, order a bagel and coffee, and scan the help-wanted ads. But he never got past the headlines.

The victim was thirty years old. He was a local kid, went to Stadium High. He had come back to help his mother, who was laid up with a shattered ankle.

It was late at night. The man was walking home from a party, a few miles north of Shawn's apartment. Two black kids asked him for a cigarette. When he reached into his pocket to get one, he was struck down from behind. A group of eight kids, aged 11 to 19, beat him to a pulp. One of them had a croquet mallet. After the victim lost consciousness, the 19-year-old performed professional wrestling-style drops, driving his knee into the man's skull. He did this more than two dozen times, counting them off as he went.

After six days in a coma, the man had passed away the previous afternoon. The police described it as a "thrill killing," and concluded that the suspects did it largely because they were bored.

Welcome to Tacoma, Shawn. Try not to get killed by the animals.

The city was holding a community forum that night at Stadium High. Shawn decided he had to go.

When he arrived at the school, about a mile from his apartment, he found a kind of castle, peppered with spires. He composed several histories in his head, but figured he would learn the real one soon. He crossed a courtyard spotted with squares of frosted glass, lit from underneath, and filed into the gym.

He sat in the back row, feeling his newcomer status. It wasn't long before the 20 rows in front of him had filled up. Dozens of latecomers were forced to stand in the back. One was an elderly woman, standing to Shawn's right, one hand on the folded-up bleachers.

She had wispy silver hair and rather astonishing blue eyes, and looked unsteady, shifting from one foot to the other. Shawn touched the woman's arm and asked her if she would take his seat.

"Thank you so much," she said. "I think that's why I don't go to art museums anymore — I literally can't stand them! Hah-hah!"

Her laughter, a two-beat hiccup, contrasted the crowd's general mood. Shawn recalled his uncle's funeral, where his uncle's best friend finished the eulogy by telling their favorite jokes.

The mayor gave a brief talk and introduced a young woman, a close friend of the victim. The news reports had hinted at the young man's character, but this first testimony expanded it profoundly.

"I feel most sorry for the world," she concluded, wiping away tears. "Because the world... has lost the kindest... most gentle human being I have ever known."

Many of the speakers ran along these lines. Some complained about the police, who had recorded a series of similar attacks but failed to report them to the affected neighborhoods. Others lamented the violent state of society at large, and a deteriorating sense of community.

At the end of two hours, Shawn didn't feel any better about the killing, but he did feel better about his neighbors. He stood outside the entrance, watching the stream of faces. One of them was the old lady, who was now making her way toward him. She walked slowly, so Shawn had time to imagine her first words.

Thanks so much for offering me your seat.

Such a shame, isn't it?

Were you a friend of his?

She arrived a few seconds later, and put a hand on Shawn's arm.

"Do you paint?"

Buttermilk

Shawn put on a rain jacket and set out for Shelly Norman's. The address was Stadium Way, so he decided to head for the high school and figure it out from there. In the light of day, he was able to re-appraise the architecture. The spires became pyramidal gables topped with Russian-looking ornaments, bronze gone spearmint green with patina. The externals were a matter of three stripes: steep wooden roofs, two stories of thin, flame-colored bricks, and a five-foot base of rough-cut sandstone.

A plaque in the courtyard explained the materials as windfalls from Tacoma's long-standing international port — bricks from China, sandstone from Italy. It was built by the Northern Pacific Railroad as a hotel, in the style of a chateau, then abandoned during the 1893 depression and later purchased by the city.

Crossing the parking lot, Shawn peered through a high spiked fence to find the reason for the school's name: the largest high school stadium he had ever seen, set into a natural basin facing Commencement Bay. The field was artificial turf, alternating five-yard stripes of kelly and forest green, bracketed by two small mountains of concrete bleachers. The far end zone was so close to the water that a well-booted field goal could, at the moment, land on the Libyan freighter anchored on the other side.

Shawn circled the field, not realizing that he was on Stadium Way until he heard Shelly's trilled greeting.

"Shawn! Shaw-awn! Over here!"

She stood in front of a three-story Tudor with a peaked roof, decorative planking and a low covered porch. He was painting this?

"Hi," he said, climbing the steps.

"You can imagine what it's like on game nights," said Shelly. "Of course, it used to hold twenty thousand, so I shouldn't complain. Come on in! I got us some doughnuts."

Shawn had to work to keep down his salivary glands. With dwindling cash, he had yet to buy groceries. He sat at the kitchen table and dug into a jelly-filled as Shelly outlined the project.

"At the end of the driveway is my garage, which Richard converted to a studio about ten years ago. I haven't quite figured out what to do with it, but I do want to keep it in good condition, and it's looking a little doggy. You'll need to give it a good scraping first, so I got you a wire brush and a putty knife, whichever you prefer. I also got some primer, for the bare spots. That'll probably take you most of today. If we get sun tomorrow, you can start the painting then. I'll pick up the paint this afternoon. Do you like grilled cheese?"

Shawn wiped his mouth with a napkin. "Sure. Love it."

"Good! I'm not much of a cook, but when it comes to melting cheese, I'm an artist. You like Coca-Cola?"

"Sure."

"Well, there's your lunch. I'll bring it out in a couple hours. Oh, and there's a ladder next to the studio. Be careful, though — it's a little rickety. And there's a radio out there, too."

Shawn took a glazed old-fashioned to the driveway and set the ladder under the front roof beam, where constant exposure had done the most damage. He thought of his response the night before.

"Paint? I... painted my dad's tool shed."

"Would you paint for me? I'll pay you ten dollars an hour."

"Um, sure! Just so you know I'm no expert."

"Expertise is not required. A good heart, patience — that's what I need. Tomorrow at ten. Here's the address."

Working the putty knife under the more obvious flakes, Shawn was forming a plan of action. If you paint over a piece of loose paint, it will start to peel that much sooner. Therefore, you must scrape like a fascist, seeking and destroying all flaws. It almost seemed like fun.

Most of the work was on the beam, along with three sun-baked patches on the front wall (which was, essentially, the old garage door, nailed shut). After scraping, he found an old broom and ran it across the walls, cleaning out cobwebs and small flakes. Then he pulled out the primer. For this, he had a more immediate reference.

"I don't think I'm doing it right, Dad. It looks all... blotchy."

"No, no. That's fine. The primer has its own special job. It soaks into the wood and seals it off. If it looks blotchy, that just means it's working. That allows the paint to do its job, which is to cover everything and make it look pretty."

His dad stopped to scratch his moustache. "Gee. You might even say the primer is a man and the paint is a woman. But you might not understand that for a while."

Where scraping afforded the luxury of destructiveness, primer afforded the luxury of sloppiness. Shawn stirred it with a fallen twig, then used an old brush to slap it over the patches of bare wood. He had just about finished when Shelly appeared on the back steps with a paper plate and a Coke.

"Hey! Look at you! You've made good progress. Come and have some food."

"All right!" said Shawn. He cleaned the brush under the garden tap, then joined his employer on the front porch. He was surprised to find that he'd been working for four hours.

"You should have seen what Richard went through when he first painted that thing. Someone had let one of those godawful passion vines take over both sides. It took him two days of yanking and clipping to get rid of it – and then another day for scraping, cleaning and priming. Gee willikers, you were hungry, weren't you?"

Shawn had polished off the first sandwich – made with generous slabs of Swiss and cheddar – and was halfway through the second.

"I'm not much of a breakfast person," he said.

Shelly peered over Shawn's shoulder. He could see the skyscape that made her eyes so interesting: a mottling gray that gave them the appearance of blue opals.

"I'll tell you what," she said. "The way those clouds look, I'm thinking you should leave the actual painting for tomorrow. I am, however, going to pay you in advance, on the condition that you get to a tire store and replace that nitro-glycerin spare. I don't want you running off a road somewhere and leaving my poor studio half-done."

She handed Shawn a fold of cash. He thanked her, and slid it into his pocket, thinking it rude to count it in front of her. When he looked back up, she was staring at a spot across the street.

"Richard certainly loved those football games."

When he reached the far side of the school, Shawn took out the cash and counted 124 dollars. An hour later, the guy at the used-tire place let out a low whistle.

"I'da given you maybe ten more feet before she blew."

On the way home, he had to force his body to relax. What with black dogs and exploding tires, he had taken to driving all tensed-up, prepared for calamity.

The next morning was so bright that Rainier's snowy flanks disappeared in the glare. He decided to walk to work, just to take it all in, and stopped at a coffeehouse shaped like a ski chalet. When he got to the house, Shelly proffered a trio of bear-claws and a box of supplies: a three-inch brush, stir-sticks, a key for opening paint cans, and a gallon of exterior flat the color of buttermilk.

He started from the beams, and once again began to develop a strategy. The back of the can said to brush toward the previously painted area, to avoid lap-marks. But this didn't entirely work. It didn't fill in the rough grain of the baked-out wood. He found he could apply a number of strokes in the opposite direction, as long as the final stroke was back toward the paint. As the hours passed, his brushwork became increasingly fluid, and he sensed that he might have a talent for this.

By lunchtime (grilled Muenster on sourdough), he had finished the roof beams and front wall. He did the side walls during the afternoon, and by four-thirty was standing in the pre-dusk light, admiring his crisp white structure. He was especially proud of the beams, which betrayed nary a sign of their previous neglect. He heard the kitchen door creak open behind him.

"Goodness!" Shelly half-sang. "A Michelangelo in the making. I don't think Richard would even recognize it."

He assumed, from her constant references, that Shelly's husband had died fairly recently. She spoke of him as if he were still around.

"I know I paid you in advance," she said. "But it looks so splendid, I want you to take this twenty and have some fun tonight. Then, on Monday, we can start the kitchen."

Wheat

Nothing burns a hole in your pocket like a twenty-dollar bill with instructions. Shawn took a bath, missing two streaks of paint in his hair, then slipped on some Levi's and a semi-clean shirt and headed downtown.

Halfway down St. Helens Avenue he found himself in a crowd, outside a coffeehouse called Mocha Mountain. Next door was a dark room, tables and chairs packed around a modest stage. A clean-cut guitarist in a suede ballcap stood behind the mic, playing a revved-up version of "All Along the Watchtower."

He was followed by a hepcat with a single-tuft goatee on the end of his chin. He paid appropriate compliments to the guitarist, then eyed a list of names and smiled.

"Prepare yourself," he said, "for the female tsunami of poetry... our own Ivy Listrom!"

The woman who rose from the table next to Shawn's didn't take the stage so much as commandeer it. She was a collection of earth-mother curves that didn't quite meet at the seams. Her face was hard to organize, too: a proud left-leaning nose, balanced by a golden stud above her right nostril; wheat-colored hair, braided back to highlight a broad, smooth forehead, lush, expressive lips and round, ice-blue eyes.

She greeted the applause with a wide, surprising smile. She dwindled it with a brief flurry of Hindu-like dance steps, then wiped it out by circling her hip and stomping the stage. She balled her fists and held them to her face, then fanned her fingers to either side and spoke calmly, tasting each syllable.

"The name is Tahoma," she said. "Ta. Ho. Ma. Write that down. Some have forgotten it, which doesn't please me as - much - as - it - might."

She then took a slow spin, her arms ghosting a spiral orbit, and looked at the audience as if she'd just discovered them.

"It was given to me by the people you call Native Americans. They really haven't been around all that long – not in *my* kind of time – but I grew to like them. They didn't ask for much. A few trout from my streams, a few sticks of wood for the fire. I gave them that sense of connection, the ice-music that played down their spines when they caught sight of my snow-white flanks. You could even say they feared me."

Big, satisfied CEO smile.

"I like that."

Laughter. Ivy paced, reassessing the room.

"Then came Vancouver. British explorer. They named an island after him. He sailed his little raft into the sound, took a look at my awesome crest and said, 'My, what a lovely mountain. I shall name it after my friend Rainier, the rear admiral.'"

Pause. Deadpan gaze.

"Let me repeat that. Rear. Admiral. Rear."

Angry squint.

"That *really* pissed me off."

A guy in the back shouts, "Yeah!"

"The ones who came later... they tried to make amends. They named your little town after me. But they threw in a 'c.' Ta-kkhoma. What is that? Yiddish?"

"They had other bad habits. Cutting down my trees. Killing off the members of my tribe. Cluttering my waterfront with buildings and freeways. And what the fuck is that smell from the paper mills?"

Pause. Thoughtful sigh. Slingshot cocking of the hips.

"I've had enough. I'm done with you assholes. I've got a little... trick I do. It's called a lahar. A lahar is a mudflow — a one hundred mile-per-hour, twenty-five-foot-high mudflow, like a wall... of liquid... cement, caused by the eruption and subsequent collapse of a volcano.

"And don't think I won't do it. You've heard of the Osceola Mudflow? I took two thousand feet off my own head for that one, and I only did it 'cause the asteroid killed off the fucking dinosaurs and I was bored, man!"

Pause. She folds her arms, businesslike.

"So what does this mean for you? First off, you can kiss all your river towns goodbye. Buckley? Buckled. Enumclaw? Clawed out. Puyallup. Pewed all up. Nothing left all the way to Takkhoma, and there at the front, one of my courageous warriors, riding that twenty-five-foot wave in a dugout canoe, shouting 'Ta-ho-ma! Ta-ho-ma! Ta-ho-ma!'"

Ivy punches her syllables until the room shouts along: "Ta-ho-ma! Ta-ho-ma!" She lets it ride for twenty seconds, then cuts them off with a sweep of her hand. She lets the silence fester, and then sneaks up on the mic.

"Do not fuck... with the name... of a mountain."

Ivy accepted the applause and then headed outside for a smoke. The next performer was a red-haired high-school girl who sat at the upright and played Rachmaninoff, but Shawn was too distracted to listen. He picked his way outside, where the hepcat emcee was engaging Ivy in debate.

"But really, Ivy, why would a mountain care what you called it? Rainier exists in geological time. We're nothing, man! Gnats! Little, tiny gnats."

Ivy laughed. "Jesus, Jud! It's just for fun. It's just... rhetorical! Lighten up."

Shawn butted his way in and extended a hand.

"Hi, Ivy. I'm Shawn. That was great!"

"Thanks," said Ivy, with a practiced smile. She was used to compliments.

"You know what it needs, though?"

"No," said Ivy, laughing. "What does it need?"

"Drums," said Shawn. "It needs drums."

Raw Sienna

Shelly had gone all out: a Rueben on Jewish rye, loaded with sauerkraut. Shawn spent half his lunch wiping the juice from his chin as he tried to tell a story.

"So Ivy came to my apartment for a rehearsal."

"Oh!" said Shelly. "Any romantic possibilities?"

Shawn laughed. "You cut right to the chase, don't you?"

"I'm old. I have to."

"No," Shawn answered. "Ivy has an obsession for black guys with dreadlocks and round spectacles."

"So... she's looking for Bobby McFerrin?"

"Could I please get back to the story?"

"By all means."

"Thank you. So we tried out the Tahoma thing with every last piece of my drum kit, but we couldn't get the right sound. Ivy decided what we needed was congas — and said she had a friend who could bring some to the reading. Problem was, come Thursday night, Ivy's friend failed to show."

"Did he have dreadlocks?"

"Huh?"

"Ivy's friend."

"No. But he did have an old car, which broke down, leaving us without drums. We were pacing around the back room at Mocha Mountain when I picked up a cardboard box and started slapping it. It had a pretty good tone. I found a big aluminum spoon to add volume, and that's how I made my debut."

"How beautifully primitive!" said Shelly. "Did it work?"

"Yes. With one surprise. I failed to notice that the box was half-full of Styrofoam packing peanuts. When I started applying the spoon with great force – about the spot in the poem when the volcano erupts – the peanuts started poofing out the top like little spurts of magma."

"Hah!" said Shelly. "A multi-media performance."

"Poor Ivy. She had no idea why she was getting laughs in all the wrong places."

Shawn had worked on the kitchen for four days — although he had cut his workdays to six hours. Shelly treated him like a houseguest, and could only maintain that level of attentiveness for so long.

The project was pretty complicated. Houses near the sound were susceptible to settling, creating lots of cracks that needed to be spackled. Then he had to apply two coats of primer behind the stove, where the wall was stained by heat and grease.

Shawn was fascinated by the rolling process – its sheer efficiency – but then came the windows. There were four, each with two sets of quarter-framed panes. Shawn painted them freehand, bending his body at odd angles to keep the brush from slopping on the glass.

The final element was an old-fashioned telephone nook that Shelly had reserved for a porcelain angel inherited from her mother. Shawn had to yank out the old phone lines, sand down their tracks, then apply several coats of white semi-gloss until it gave forth a suitably sacred glow.

He stepped back to take in the whole kitchen, as white and clean as the inside of an igloo. He looked out the window to see Shelly, lugging some large object out of the studio, and headed out to help.

"Go ahead," she said, winded from the effort. "Open it up."

Shawn loosened the plastic covering and worked it over the sides of a conga drum — varnished blonde wood, stainless steel fittings, cappuccino skin tight across the rims.

"It's beautiful."

"It's Richard's," said Shelly. "Now it's yours."

Shawn was so excited about his new toy that he called Ivy and insisted on a rehearsal. Previously, he had simply followed the peaks and valleys of the volcano's temper. Now he was able to work in some tricks. Ivy suggested a rim shot at Vancouver's entrance, and a questioning triplet at the first mention of the lahar. Shawn threw in three dramatic cutoffs for Tahoma's stern asides. But the most powerful moment was already there — the final passage, when Shawn would work up a blizzard of beats and then drop it off a cliff at Ivy's signal. The silence would leave people holding their breaths and not knowing why.

He had learned a few things about Ivy. She had just come home after earning a theater arts degree at NYU. Her dad was a doctor who played trombone in a jazz trio. Ivy worked at his office, saving up for an attack on Los Angeles.

They decided to take their new "Tahoma" to Shakabrah, a coffeehouse diner in the 6th Street district. The place had a spacious side-room that hosted regular acoustic concerts and, every Saturday, an open mic. After their sound check, Shawn retreated to a table at the back wall while Ivy went to the door and hugged every other person who entered.

With the side-room curtained off, Shawn had but a small square of vision into the street: through the coffeehouse door and over a table full of diners. This was where she appeared. A streetlight switched on across the road, hanging like a star over her shoulder.

The most striking thing was the contrast of her features: a shroud of black hair, big dark eyes and scarlet lipstick on a canvas of cream-white skin. She held a navy blue overcoat against her neck and peered anxiously down the street.

And then, she slipped from the frame. Shawn blinked, and returned to his newspaper. He looked up once in a while when a new figure entered the room: a poet with a fistful of papers, a guitarist lugging an amplifier. The room filled up fast. Ivy was content to roam, chatting up this table and that before settling at the side of the stage with a pageboy redhead.

And then she was there again, standing in the doorway. The only seat left was across from Shawn, and that's where she went. She arrived with a shy but astonishing smile.

"Would it be all right if I sat here?"

"Certainly," Shawn said. "Sure."

The long woolen coat gave her the aura of a Russian princess. She draped it over her stool and perched on top. Shawn could not even guess how to start a conversation, until she set down a book like a big fat cue card.

"Nabakov! Are you far into it?"

"Yes," she said. "It's downright scary how good he is. You find yourself almost rooting for the protagonist, and then you think, 'Wait a minute. The protagonist is a child molester!'"

"Not to mention, he's writing in his second language. If I could put three words together like that in any language..."

"Dostoyevsky's my favorite, though. That sneaky sense of humor. I just finished *The Brothers Kara*..."

"Really? I had a hard time getting through..."

"Oh! It's all in the translation. They get too academic sometimes and it dries right up. I'll loan you my copy sometime."

Jesus, thought Shawn. *She's already loaning me books.* He was about to introduce himself when he was interrupted.

"Greetings!" It was Amy, the pageboy redhead, halfway swallowing the mic. "Welcome to this week's edition of Shaaah-kabrah! Let's begin with Angie, who will seduce you with songs of torturous, sadistic love. Applause!"

Angie's quiet guitar forced them into courteous silence, but they shared whispered comments during the applause. The nice part was having to lean his face close to hers in order to be heard.

"She's quite good," he said.

"Yeah. But she sounds too much like..."

"Definitely. She was better on that original."

"We should tell her that," she said. "You know, in a nice way."

Two singers and a poet later, Amy introduced Ivy.

"And I have it on good information," she added, "that Ivy's drummer has graduated from cardboard boxes to actual percussion instruments!"

Shawn gave the princess a sheepish grin and headed for the stage, arranging his stool and conga as Ivy gave some introductory comments. Fortunately, he had an internal switch that shut out distractions, and he quickly became absorbed in the performance.

Ivy was more electric than ever, causing Shawn to drive up the volume a little too quickly. By mid-lahar, he was pounding the shit out of his stick-soft hands. The final cut seemed to swallow the room, which then imploded in a burst of hoots and shouts. They were, officially, a hit.

And what a great way to impress a woman you've just met, thought Shawn. He stood to absorb the applause, gave Ivy a pat on the shoulder, and then returned to his table.

Her eyes were flashing with raw sienna, and he realized her face came from another time: Claudette Colbert, or Marilyn Monroe.

"Woo!" she said. "That was fantastic!"

Thanks," he said. "I suppose I should have warned you."

The next performer was a burly guitarist with a gravelly bass voice, a little like Tom Waits. Shawn didn't hear much, because he was trying to work up his nerve. He just had to ask her out, but they really hadn't talked much, and why was this so goddamned difficult? His muteness extended through the next two songs, after which the princess stood to put on her coat. Shawn experienced an immediate internal panic.

She leaned over to talk into his ear.

"I need to get up ridiculously early tomorrow. But here, give me a call."

She slipped a business card into his hand and left, stopping at the door to send him a wave, rolling her fingers against her palm. Shawn gave a courteous salute, and she was gone.

The American flag stood atop City Hall, in a spotlight at the center of his cityscape, snapping courageously in a fierce storm-front wind. Shawn knelt at his window, rubbing his sore hands, thinking, *It must be glorious up there.*

He reached for his bass drum/nightstand and picked up the card for the fiftieth time that night. Tacoma Davenport. Perhaps this is how you fall in love with a woman, a little bit at a time.

Black

Shawn found himself attracting odd people. First was the wiry black guy by the apartment dumpster, who decided he just had to give Shawn a full account of his morning discoveries. ("See? You glue that earpiece on and these here, they work just fine!") And within a block, two different men asked him for cigarettes, and then some Asian lady asked him for directions, outlining the address on her hand.

The prize character came at a Starbucks near UW-Tacoma: a large, athletic man in his mid-thirties who sat reading a textbook. He wore a black biker vest outlined in squares of silver and turquoise, and a headband of silver circles over his long, blond hair. He ran a finger over the text and recited pieces of it in a calm baritone, as if he were giving instructions to a young dog.

"My words... foment... much danger, remember? I can shatter your ulcers... assassination... Watch this missile... CIA — I've seen your computers, too... The archangel is circumnavigating... statement... see how you rebuilt cocaine reduction? Let me give a warning to all nations: you do not question God."

Ah, thought Shawn. *Religion and conspiracy theories: the principal indicators of mental disease.*

"The CIA has cookies!"

Not that Shawn much cared. He had a date. Strolling back through the grand old buildings of downtown, he began to understand what had drawn him here. Tacoma was a town with holes to be filled, spaces to be used. He passed the construction site for the new art museum, saw a sign for a proposed shopping center, looked across the water where the

Museum of Glass Art was rising from its foundation. The whole town seemed to be preparing for some economic messiah, and he was happy to dig out a spot and wait for deliverance.

Shawn climbed Market Street and passed a vacant bank, wrought-iron chandeliers hanging from high ceilings, green and blue tiles trimming the facade. It cried out for a restaurant or nightclub. He'd open it himself if he could.

But first, he had a date.

They sat on a velvet bench in the lobby, sneaking bites of popcorn, waiting for the movie to get out. Rivulets of rain shifted on the window as Tacoma answered the obvious question.

"My mom's first marriage lasted a year — precisely. She left on their anniversary. When the divorce came through, she took a flight to Los Angeles, rented a car and drove up the coast. She ran out of land at Cape Flattery, Washington, where she met my father. He was on a post-divorce getaway himself, having driven all the way from the south hills of Pittsburgh. Which is precisely where my mother grew up.

"They figured it was fate. They were wrong. They drove back to the south hills and got married. When I came along, eight months after the marriage (I'll let you figure that one out), they picked a name from the state where they met. I'm damn lucky they didn't call me Spokane."

"Or Federal Way," Shawn said with a grin.

"Yeah. So, about a year ago, for lots of reasons, I decided that it was my turn to flee to the West Coast, and figured, I'm named after the place — why not here?"

"Good as any place," Shawn said. "But... you don't give this lengthy explanation to everyone, do you?"

"Mom and Dad were hippies."

"That works."

"Oh, look — movie's out." She took Shawn's hand and led him into the theater.

The movie was about a children's board game that kept whipping up disastrous enchantments: sudden floods, invasions of frogs. Shawn cringed at the extended screams – Hollywood's latest overdone gag – but did enjoy its unusually dark edge. At times, you weren't even sure if all the principals would survive. Not that Shawn much cared. He was lost in the light-finger dance of Tacoma's hand in his, and the pillow of black curls against his shoulder.

When Shawn was extremely happy, he tended to ramble. All the way back to Tacoma's house, he gave the movie a thorough going-over, surprised at how much he liked it after the fact. Pulling up to her curb, he realized he had cowed her into silence.

"You know, it's all right if you didn't like it. It ain't *Casablanca*. C'mon, tell me what you think."

She smiled sheepishly (come to think of it, she always smiled sheepishly). "Well, it was entertaining. I thought the actors did a great job, and the special effects were amazing."

"Out with it!" said Shawn.

"Okay. It's just that all that witchcraft bugged me. You see, I'm a pretty serious Christian, and that stuff kinda creeps me out. It's almost like... devil worship.

"Plus, it's... Something happened to me in Seattle. I went to a health store up there, in the Fremont district, to get this special ginseng tea. This strange man was there, he was sort of... impish. He had yellow teeth, and you could almost see the horns sprouting from his head. He got all pissed off at me, for no reason, and I'm convinced he put something evil in my tea, because for the next two days I couldn't think straight, like there was something fogging my thoughts. And I saw... visions. I haven't been back to Seattle since. I'm convinced that impish little man is after me. Oh, I..."

She could see how hard Shawn was trying to follow her story.

"I'm sorry." She let out a nervous laugh. "This is hardly the thing to talk about on a first date!"

What she didn't know was that Shawn was fully occupied watching her lips move, and figuring out how he was going to get around to kissing her.

"Thanks for the movie," she said. She leaned over and kissed him on the lips. "Give me a call soon."

He watched her walk away.

Shawn didn't feel the spider-strings of dread until the next day, walking the seawall at Point Defiance, studying bits of poetry etched into the sidewalk. Then he was back on Wendy Fisher's couch, doing the nightly dry-hump while the Rev and his wife snoozed away upstairs. He reached up the back of Wendy's blouse and tried to undo her bra. Wendy grabbed his hand and held it out like a dead rat.

"You just don't get it, do you, Shawn? Sex is not a plaything. It is a holy sacrament. God does not intend for us to partake of it until we are married. So stop it!"

Shawn had suffered two years of this treatment, in the hopes that one day Wendy's constant horniness would drive her over the edge. But that night, the final tumbler clicked into place and he could see the Christian trap for what it was. He shot up from the couch, his erection tenting his jeans.

"Fuck your god, Wendy! Your god pumped you so full of chemicals you're down here every night using me like some fucking human trampoline. And then he tells you you're evil for doing it. Your god is a pansy-ass pricktease, Wendy, and so are you! I'm leaving."

Wendy's shock turned quickly to sobbing, and for all the wrong reasons. She was petrified that her parents had heard Shawn's tirade, that her evil urges would finally be found out. But her parents were engaged in boisterous canine sex, and wouldn't have noticed if Billy Graham walked in for a personal sermon.

Wendy also didn't know that Shawn wasn't just leaving her. He was leaving Ellensburg.

"Centaur Systems."

"Hi Tacoma."

"Well hi." Tacoma's business voice melted like butter. "How are you today?"

"I... um, I wanted to tell you something. I was thinking about what you said last night, and I thought it only fair to tell you: I'm not a Christian. I thought I should tell you right away, because I thought maybe you might be looking for a Christian guy."

Shawn had bolstered himself for any number of hurt responses, but not for what he got: the kind of lilting sigh one emits at the sight of a cute puppy-dog.

"Oh, that is so sweet! That is so considerate. But no, it's okay, really. I'm not necessarily... exclusive that way."

"Oh. Okay."

"So were you calling just for that, or were you going to ask me out?"

"Oh, um — sure! What would you like to do?"

"How about a drive? I've been dying to see Port Townsend."

They talked for another half-hour, about whatever they could think of, completely distracting Tacoma from her Saturday work session. After a dozen variations on "Goodbye" and "See you soon," Shawn hung up, thinking, *Oh man. I've got a live one here.*

Blue-White

They drove through beautiful farmland valleys on their way to Port Townsend, bathed in rare February sunlight all the way. Shawn ambled the old brick storefronts of town, Tacoma tucked into his shoulder, the smells of grilled seafood and saltwater taffy filling his nose.

Port Townsend's north-south bearing offered a clear choice of sides: sunny or shady. Shawn and Tacoma joined the 80 percent who chose the former. Tacoma was most interested in curios and furnishings, determined to liven up her drab apartment. She stopped at a framed print, a Japanese girl in traditional white makeup and kimono, reclining on a settee.

"She's just gorgeous, don't you think?"

"Sure."

"I've always had a fascination with Oriental women. They have a kind of serenity that American women don't."

"Especially Pennsylvanian women," said Shawn.

Tacoma gave him a pinch in the ribs. "Just for that, I'm getting it. And I'm making you carry it."

They bought ice cream cones and took them to a used bookstore. Tacoma went straight to Russian literature.

"I never got around to telling you – that memorable night we met – but I was a Russian major in college. Omigod! Look at this."

She pulled out an old book with black leather binding and gold Russian letters.

"Nikolay Gogol," she said, flipping the pages. "My God, that smell! They should put that in a bottle and call it 'Old Book.'"

"Speaking of the night we met," said Shawn. "What were you looking so anxious about?"

"Oh! I was looking for my friend Terry. It was her idea to go to the open-mic that night, but then she got the stomach flu and was too busy throwing up to call me."

"Send her my thanks."

"Sure. Ouch! Thirty bucks."

"Little rich forya?"

"It's just that I've read it in English already. Seems like kind of a waste."

"Let me get half of it."

"Oh, well, I didn't mean to..."

"Don't worry. I've got a nice painting job right now. Just so long as you read some of it to me."

"Oh," said Tacoma. "So you're one of those, are you?"

"One of whats?"

"Some guys get off on women who speak Russian."

"No kidding!"

"Yep."

"So say something."

"Shto-NO-vava."

"Yeah, that's kinda fun. What's it mean?"

"How's it hangin'?"

"That the Bronx translation?"

"Nah. Picksburgh — where we take the 'T' dawn-tawn 'n' eat pirogies 'n' pop 'n'at. What's so funny? They really talk like that."

Shawn was trying to fight a laugh. "Not that," he said. "I was just thinking of one of my sicker fantasies."

"Well! You're gonna have to tell me now."

"Okay. Having, um... relations with a woman while she speaks to me in a language other than English."

Tacoma cultivated a wicked smile, her eyes tick-tocking back and forth like a retro cat-clock.

"Wha...?" asked Shawn.

"Shto-NO-vava," she said.

"Shto-NO-vava," he repeated.

"Good! We'll teach you more later."

Shawn hated backtracking, so he had worked out a loop, across Whidbey Island and back through Seattle. They waited in the ferry line for 45 minutes. Tacoma read him a chapter of Russian, then stretched out to rest her head in Shawn's lap. Once on the ferry, they climbed up top to watch a bank of clouds drift over the Olympics and drown out the sun.

They drove up Whidbey Island to Deception Pass, where a high bridge joins the island to the mainland. They walked across to watch the wild currents below, then hiked to a beach of smooth stones the size of coffee coasters. Shawn stood and watched the water, which flowed left-to-right in front of him, but right-to-left on the far side. He found a good stone and winged it sidearm. It left a dozen dimples and sank, fifty feet away. He felt hands wrapping him from behind.

"You're good at everything, aren't you?"

"Just try me."

"I will. What the hell is that?"

She stared at the top of a Douglas fir.

"Bald eagle," Shawn said. "They're so thick around here, you gotta beat 'em off with a stick."

"And there's another."

"Really?"

"Just past the first one, up and to the left."

Just then, the two birds took off in tandem, cruising over the water to the meeting point of the currents. The larger one dropped, dipping its claws into the water but coming up empty. They returned to their treetops, unfazed.

"Can I breathe now?" said Tacoma.

"No," Shawn answered, and then he did something he'd never thought to do — peeling back her fingers like the petals of a flower, he kissed the palm of her hand. Her smile drained all the light from the overcast.

"Thank you," she said.

Driving the dark stretches toward Seattle, Shawn was feeling drowsy. Tacoma saw him shaking his eyes, and ran a finger along his shoulder.

"Sleepy?"

"Yeah."

"Here," she said. "I brought something for entertainment." She pulled a cassette from her purse and slipped it into Shawn's deck. It was Tacoma's voice.

"So tell me about Vaudeville, Grandma."

What came out next was the voice of a charming witch — the one who feeds you candy right before popping you into the oven.

"Oh! It was wonderful. Heeeh! You never knew who was gonna be big someday. I was on a bill with Allen and Burns one week, and they had this good-looking tie salesman who was always tagging along. His name was Archie Leach. Years later, he changed it to Cary Grant."

The Tacoma on the tape let out a squeal of laughter.

"Mind you," said Grandma. "I was no big deal, showgirl mostly, one time a magician's assistant. But I was a stunner, honey, and I got invited to a lot of parties. One time I went to a big tuh-doo at the Carnegie mansion, and there was this big palooka following me around. I tried to shake him by going out to the garden, but there he was, right behind me like my shadow. So I just told him, flat-out, that I was a good Italian girl, and if I was ever gonna sacrifice my virtue it wouldn't be for an ugly mug like himself. Hah! He stomped away, and I never saw him again. Well the next day, my best gal Trudy informs me that I had just put the damper on Babe Ruth! Well! I don't care how many run-homes a guy hits, if he looks like that he can just forget it."

Tape Tacoma let out a generous roll of laughter, while live Tacoma whispered footnotes. "I recorded this just before I left Pittsburgh. Grandma was pretty sick, and I just wanted to make sure I..."

"Gracie Allen introduced me to Flo Ziegfield once," said Grandma. "And Ziegfield invited me to New York for an audition, but my mother she... she..." She finished the sentence in a plaintive cry. "She wouldn't let me!"

Tacoma hit the eject button.

"I'm sorry. I forgot that was coming. All her stories end up at Flo freakin' Ziegfield. And that seventy-year-old bitterness... it gets worse with age. You see, my mom had a lot of problems when I was twelve, so I went to live with Grandma. She did a pretty good job, I guess, but when I got back from college she still insisted on running every five minutes of my life. That's why I left. Change of subject? Please?"

"Even better," said Shawn. He spotted a rest area and pulled in. They took their respective pit stops, and then met at the water fountain. Shawn pulled her to a picnic bench, away from the lights.

"Well," said Tacoma. "What could you have in mind?"

Shawn gave her a long kiss, then said, "But that's not all. Do you know Orion?"

"Orion?"

He pointed behind her to the southwest sky.

"Oh! Orion."

"Wanted to show you a little trick I learned in Boy Scouts." He turned her around and extended an arm over her shoulder. "See the foot down there? That's Rigel. Rigel is Arabic for 'foot.' Go figger. Now the head up there? Sorta reddish? That's Betelgeuse. Now. Start at Rigel, then head straight through Betelgeuse until you hit something."

"Little star there?"

"Nope. Go further."

"Two big stars."

"Right! That's Castor on the right, Pollux on the left. The twins of Gemini."

"Ah."

"Now. Go back to Betelgeuse."

"Red."

"Then straight through the right-hand shoulder and..."

"Bright star!"

"That's Aldebaran, the brightest star of Taurus. If you keep going you'll hit the Pleiades. Now! Orion's belt, right to left: Mintaka, Alnilam, and... Alnitak. The Arabs call them 'the golden nuts.'"

"Like to meet a man with golden nuts."

"I should've seen that coming. Now! Follow the belt right to left and keep going."

"'Nother bright star, right... there."

"Righteous! Any guesses?"

"The Starship Enterprise?"

"Sirius. The Dog Star. Canis Major. Brightest damn star in the sky."

"Woof! So Orion is like a big roadmap to the stars."

"Yep! Ready for the freeway?"

"One more kiss."

It wasn't as hard to stay awake after that, and soon they were pulling up to Tacoma's house. She asked him in for coffee. They climbed a side stairwell to her apartment and walked the long hall to her room. She had a large window overlooking the front yard, and a ceiling that angled down at either side, giving the room a cozy geometry. Tacoma hit a button on her stereo, and turned to Shawn with a smile.

"Dance?"

He seemed to remember something about coffee, but didn't mind, standing and wrapping an arm about her waist. The stereo played a country ballad with a distorted edge — a lazy strum, a woman's voice full of bending. They swayed together, well-matched, and Shawn turned to kiss her cheek. He realized it was a breakup song, full of goodbyes and closing doors.

"Who is this?"

"Mazzy Star."

"Never heard of her. But I like."

"I'll make you a tape."

She offered to give him a neckrub. He sat on the floor as she perched behind him on her futon, digging into his shoulders till he was all rubbery. When he offered to return the favor, she removed her blouse and bra, revealing generous milk-white breasts.

It seemed too casual to be an invitation. Even if it had been, he wouldn't have taken it. Because this is how you fall in love with a woman, a little bit at a time. He sat behind her and laid his fingers across her shoulder blades.

She turned her head half-around and asked him to pull her hair – then asked him to pull harder. Once he reached the desired torque, her eyes squinted in pleasure and her smile rose up in the blue light of the stereo.

She asked him to stay and sleep, which he did, surprised at his ability to hold his charges. She kissed him awake at sunrise, whispering of bagels on the counter, and that long-promised coffee.

Shamrock

The color was blood red. The company called it New England Brick, but to Shawn it could have come straight from the vein. He daubed his brush, riffled one side against the can, and pulled it along the baseboard. He wiped up a drop with his finger, and it looked like he had just cut himself.

By lunchtime, he had worked the edges all the way around the hall. The doors were left for other exotics: raspberry and burnt sienna. Shawn enjoyed the double crackle of his sandwich, bacon on Dutch crunch bread (Swiss cheese in between).

"Mmmf! You've outdone yourself."

"I'm thinking of opening a deli," she said, getting that bemused nebula in her eyes. "So are you going to tell me, or do I have to whack you over the head with a skillet?"

"What?"

"The performance! How did it go?"

"Oh, sorry." Shawn let out a shy smile. "I'm a bit distracted. I met a girl."

"So! Your drumming *was* good."

"Yeah. She liked the way my hands worked, the way I focused on my partner and stayed in synch."

"Smart girl. What's her name?"

"Tacoma."

"You're dating the city?"

"Her parents were hippies."

"Oh."

"She's pretty incredible, Shelly. And gorgeous. I can't quite get over that. There's a catch, of course. She's a Christian girl. I haven't had much luck with Christian girls."

"You've done all right with me," Shelly said, and smiled.

"Oh!" said Shawn. "I'm sorry, I..."

"'Course I came round to it in an odd way. My husband was into eastern philosophies, so I splashed around in Zen, Feng Shui, tai-chi. We were always about ten years ahead of the curve on that stuff, so we got a reputation as the neighborhood wackos. But these days, I'm right back to Episcopalian. Even go to church once in a while, just to sing the old hymns."

"I could handle Episcopalian," said Shawn. "But I always get these 'bumper sticker' Christians. You know, *Honk If You Love Jesus*, 'personal relationship with Christ.' Tacoma's not bad, but once in a while she says something like 'devil-worship,' and it freaks me out."

"Is she pushing it on you?"

"No. That's what makes it complicated. She doesn't hold non-believer status as a disqualification."

"Oh, Shawn. Don't think yourself into a corner. It's called infatuation. The two of you are going to be perfect beings for a while. Enjoy!"

Shawn gave her a nod as he took another loud bite out of his sandwich. "Speaking of impetuous behavior, what's the deal with these colors?"

"Yes! Isn't it wonderful? I always wanted a wild, bohemian household, but Francis was a bit stuffy that way."

"Oh. Who's Francis?"

"Francis is my husband, Shawn. Passed away about twenty years ago, poor soul. Smoked those damn cigarettes."

"Then... who's Richard?"

"Richard's my son."

"Oh. Then Richard passed away, too?"

Shelly blinked her eyes. "No. Richard's alive."

"Oh," said Shawn, still confused. "But it seemed like... you were talking about him... as if he were dead."

Shelly's native cheerfulness flushed from her face. She looked at her hands, gathered in her lap.

"Richard's in... prison, dear. He came back to Tacoma about ten years ago. Was always in trouble, that one. He said he could make a new start if I let him convert the garage to a studio. Give him enough space to be... independent."

She stopped and took a long breath.

"He was running a lab, Shawn. Methamphetamines. He was selling it to... kids at the high school. His best... market... was game nights at the stadium. That's when they caught him. I was used to bright lights and noise on Friday nights, but then I saw that some of the lights were from police cars. When I stepped outside, they had Richard in handcuffs, kneeling on the sidewalk. There was a big crowd of people just... staring. I never felt so stupid in all my life.

"That's why I went to that memorial service, Shawn. The night I met you. I know what it's like to lose a son."

Shawn wished he knew Shelly better, so he could offer a hug, or comforting words. Instead, he just sat, stock-still.

Shelly rose and headed to the kitchen. "You finish your sandwich, dear. I'm going to fix myself some tea."

Shawn finished his lunch, then returned to the hallway, poured the red paint in a pan, and dipped his roller.

The next day, the roller-strokes were showing through. So Shawn laid down a second coat. Shelly seemed less talkative than usual, and at lunchtime she begged off to take a nap upstairs. He arrived home at dusk, flecks of red on his hands and face, and played back a phone message from Ivy.

"Shawn! Dude! Call me right away. I got a cool new project, and I need you in on it."

He would have to stick with the snare-drum shuffle ("Ballroom Blitz") longer than he wanted ("Radar Love") because once he came off of it ("Helen, Hell on Wheels") there weren't many other directions he could go. He drove it through three verses and halfway through Pancho's guitar solo before he shifted to the ride cymbal, laying double smacks on the snare to keep the swing. When Ivy came back in on vocals, Shawn caught Jimmy sliding in a pair of triplets on rhythm guitar and matched him on the crash. Jimmy grinned. Two measures later, the song clunked to a halt like a choked-off motor. Bobby clamped a hand over his bass and quizzed Pancho.

"Is this a fast-change?"

"Yeah." Pancho played the chords as he spoke. "You got the one to the four, back to the one... four again, then the five-four-one at the turn."

Jimmy pointed at the new drummer and said, "Whattya think, Shawn?"

"Well," said Shawn, rubbing a stick along his jawline. "Let me see if I've got all this. You got a three-beat countoff, twelve-bar intro, three rounds of a twelve-bar chorus combined with a four-measure stop-verse, a twenty-four solo from Pancho there, back to the stop-verse, chorus, repeat, and then it all goes to hell."

The band stared at him.

"Boys," said Bobby. "We got us a drummer who actually counts!"

"Drummer, hell," said Jimmy. "He's a moo-sician! Where did you pick up fancy terms like 'bar' and 'chorus'?"

"The job of the drummer," said Shawn, "is to understand the structure of the song, and to guide the rest of the band along that structure."

"I told you he was good," Ivy said.

"Hey Jimmy," said Shawn. "Are you going to do that little slide on the chorus and repeat? If you are, I can smack the downbeat to set it off a little."

"Actually, no. Let's save it for the repeat, and then for the twelve-bar solo Pancho was supposed to play right after."

"I was?" said Pancho.

"Tell you what else," Shawn said. "Let's follow that with a twelve-bar drum break. You guys sketch the chords, sorta 'Wipeout'-style, and I'll fill in the gaps."

"You got it, bro," said Pancho. "But first, let's figure out this ending. Ivy, can you hit the CD again?"

After the guitarists loaded up and left, Shawn sat with Ivy on her back-porch swing. She lived on a hillside in Puyallup, overlooking a large cemetery and, further on, the speckled houselights of the Puyallup Valley.

"One helluva place you got here, Ivy."

"Yeah. Too bad I have to move."

"Really? Why?"

"The folks I live with are moving out, getting a little love-nest in Steilacoom. I'm getting a room in Tacoma, but there's no place to rehearse."

"Hmm," said Shawn. "I might have an alternative. I'll check it out and get back to you. Got a cigarette?"

"Since when do you smoke?"

"I smoke after sex and rehearsals."

Ivy handed him one and lit it for him. He took a puff and let it out quickly. Ivy reaffirmed her alpha-smoker status by performing the out-the-nose, into-the-mouth routine.

"This music is really fun!" said Shawn. "I didn't know blues had so much range. All I know is that interminable, crawly twelve-bar shit they play at jam sessions."

"The old wank-athon," said Ivy. "Yeah, real blues goes all over the place: shuffles, jumps, backporch Delta, maybe some swing-blues when we get good. When I get good."

"But you are, Ivy! You're about the blackest white girl I've ever seen. You got that Harlem growl."

"I have a fantasy that I am actually the product of my father's one-night stand with Etta James."

Shawn considered this as an explanation for Ivy's earth-mother hips, but knew that voicing such a thought was a strict no-no. Ivy took a drag and sprayed it over the valley like a fog bank.

"So what's up with you, drummer-boy?"

"Nothin' much."

"Horseshit. Who is she?"

Shawn couldn't help the smile bursting out over his face. "A goddess, apparently. I'm not sure that she actually exists."

"Oh! So we're into goddess territory. Good sex?"

"I'll say. And we haven't even had six yet."

Ivy crossed her eyes. "Boy, you are in love. So... you in on the band?"

"Hell yes. This is exactly what I left Ellensburg for. Get away from all those rectangular country beats. I never thought of playing blues before, but it seems to be there in my hands."

"Well, that's good," said Ivy. "'Cause we're playing Shakabrah in three weeks."

"Aigh!" Shawn half-screamed. "Are you nuts?"

"You get good by gigging," said Ivy. "My last band rehearsed for six friggin' months, polished every note to perfection — then broke up a week before our first gig. So what do we do for a name?"

"Gotta be Ivy and the Somethings. How about Ivy and the Dawgs?"

"Dogs?"

"D-A-W-G. Dawgs. Isn't that a blues thing?"

"Man. You are from Ellensburg."

"Wuhl I don't know! How about Ivy and the Horndawgs?"

"Ivy and the Corndogs."

"Ivy and her Sweet Fajitas."

"I got it!" said Ivy. "Ivy and her Swingin' Dicks"

"Pardon?"

"Yeah! And all you guys would be nicknamed 'Dick.' Shawn 'Dick' Turk. Jimmy 'Dick' Catarino."

"You realize you're pretty much ruling out gigs at Disneyland."

"Fuck Disneyland!"

"No," Shawn said. "That would be a punk band."

They laughed until Ivy started choking on her cigarette. Shawn spotted a car descending the opposite ridge, a road they called The Enchanted Parkway, and felt the pulse of the rhythm still coursing through his hands.

Shawn didn't know what to expect. Tacoma was the most feminine creature he had ever met. Each of her movements gave off a small sexual charge. But he had been down this road before, and was afraid he might be headed for a letdown. He wondered if she would start finding little ways of inserting Jesus into the conversation. He didn't want to share her with anybody.

She opened the door and flashed that drop-dead smile. She wore a black pantsuit with a checkered jacket — couldn't have looked more adorable if she had Mickey Mouse ears. He stood on the step below her and delivered a hearty lumberjack kiss. She slipped down in his arms, woozy with affection, and opened her eyes.

"Hi."

"Hi. What do you feel like doing?"

"More of this."

"That's pretty much guaranteed. But what else?"

"My housemate's gone. I've got dinner cooking."

"Really! What's on?"

"Chicken rice casserole, green beans, and, for dessert, sliced-up mango with vanilla ice cream."

"Sounds great."

"Come in. Sit on the couch. Watch TV."

Shawn watched a couple college basketball teams have at it. He took the first commercial to sneak behind her in the kitchen and wrap his arms around her waist.

"Pull my hair," she said.

He ran a hand through her fettuccine curls and tugged, evincing the familiar feline squint. After a minute, she slipped away to check the casserole and ordered him to set the table.

After the meal, he sat at the table, searching for things to say. Her silences made him nervous.

"That was great."

"Thanks." She carried her dishes to the sink.

"That cherry tree out front is going nuts."

"It's not a real cherry. They call them cherry blossom trees. They're ornamental."

More silence.

"How's work going?"

"Pretty good. I'm helping out on this huge database project, which probably means more Saturday mornings."

"That sucks."

"It's not so bad. They're paying me well."

Tacoma wiped her hands on a dishtowel and walked over to kiss him on the cheek.

"Go watch some more television. I have to go do something."

He watched a nature show about Arizona rattlesnakes. The host kept playing up their deadly venom, as if that were some kind of shocking revelation. Shawn began to feel drowsy, but then he heard footsteps in the hall. He turned to find Tacoma, wearing a silk chemise the color of shamrocks.

Red

Shawn was convinced that Tacoma was a temptress, sent by a jealous Judeo-Christian god to win him back to the fold. She was a living catalog of sexual variations, and seemed determined to make him her testing ground.

At each rendezvous, she pulled out a new set of lingerie: thongs, teddies, garter belts, bodysuits. One night she entered fully clothed, complete with overcoat and scarf, switched on some AC/DC and conducted a lengthy striptease, so thorough and professional he began to wonder about a secret past.

She bought him a porn video and gave him a complete oral treatment as he watched it. They discovered that whipped cream is splendid but chocolate syrup too sticky. They loved doing it on the living-room floor when her housemate was gone. Shawn loved it when she left on at least one article of clothing. She instructed him to grope her breasts under cover of large crowds, and he spoke of his affection for sex in the woods.

He enjoyed pleasuring her with toys, before or after. It took the pressure off, and he liked being able to sit back and watch. He found that her orgasms were quiet and many, liable to strike at any time. She discovered that she could completely paralyze him with a tongue in the ear. He bought massage oil that heated up, and spent an evening applying it at random spots along her body.

After years of focusing his lust on the female ass, he became a breast man. Given Tacoma's attributes, he didn't have much choice. He found himself thinking about them as he painted (having to be careful about standing up). He was surprised to find that Tacoma felt the same way about his butt. Friends had always ribbed him about his round cheeks – a little too shapely for a white man – and it was exactly this that she liked. Standing in the corner of Mocha Mountain one night, they both realized that she was fondling him rather overtly. She apologized; he said he didn't mind.

This was a Christian girl. Not like any he had ever met. Certainly not like Wendy Fisher. Wendy still had her effects on him. Sometimes he would blanch at his own aggressions, too accustomed to the swatting hand and the brimstone scold. He thought of asking Tacoma about the apparent conflict between her religion and her sexuality, but he was afraid to stretch his luck.

One afternoon, they were doing it doggie-style, and had managed to position themselves in front of Tacoma's full-length mirror. Shawn was fascinated by how All-American they looked, despite the bestiality of the position. Tacoma met his eyes through their reflection and smiled.

The outside world intervened soon enough. Tacoma was assigned to East Coast sales, and had to be at the office by six. After a week of nightly lovemaking, she was exhausted, so they decided to limit themselves to weekends and Wednesdays.

Shawn was disappointed, but blessed with distractions. Ivy and the Swingin' Richards (as they were finally christened) were conducting a serious cram for their gig at Shakabrah.

On the eve of their self-imposed separation, Tacoma handed him a box gift-wrapped with the Sunday comics. Inside were a copy of C.S. Lewis' *The Lion, The Witch and the Wardrobe* and a laser-pointer.

"Well, this is fun," said Shawn, spinning red circles on the wall. "What's it for?"

"I was thinking," said Tacoma, "that with our schedules, you'll be going to rehearsals about the time I'm going to bed. And I can't have you stopping in, because you'll get my motor all revved up and — rrowr-rowr!"

(The approximate sound of Mae West imitating a cat had become their euphemism for hanky-panky.)

"So here's what I want you to do. Pull up to the curb and shine this puppy through the bedroom window. I'll come out and give you a winsome smile, and then you can be on your way. And I'll feel much better."

He kissed her. "Anything else?"

"Yes." The gold in her eyes overtook the green. "I really love the cards you give me, but why do you sign them so simply?"

"Do I?"

"Yes. 'All my love, Shawn.' Save that for your grandmother, pal! I want worship. And I want you to include my name: 'For my dearest Tacoma,' blah blah blah. And date it, so I can keep track."

"I was just assuming actions speak louder..."

"Words *are* actions. Wanna see my high school yearbook?"
She handed him a thick volume with a russet cover: Mount Lebanon School for the Performing Arts.

"You never mentioned this before."

"Look. There I am."

It was a cast photo for *The Miracle Worker*. Tacoma sped through the pages, pointing out talented students – a tapdancer here, a pianist there – then showed him the star, a girl who was now on a TV sitcom. He kept spotting autographs that said *Jesus Saves* and *He is Lord*.

"So how did you go from this to a degree in Russian?"

"Lord knows. But in my screwy family it was considered a major disappointment. I guess acting just wasn't... me."

It might have been their impending separation, but that was the first night their sex felt more like lovemaking. Afterward, he tried to recount the qualities that made it seem so: a loss of self-awareness, an elevated, surrounding warmth; a tugging of fibers far beneath his skin. Just at the height, when the margins faded and the loss of existence became almost uncomfortable, Tacoma began to speak in Russian.

Yucca Spring

"Shit!"

Jimmy Catarino was having a hell of a time with the intro. The three guitarists played an opening riff while Shawn smacked hip-hop doubles on the snare. Then they would cut, count three beats (near as Shawn could tell) and come back with a trio of chords on the off-beats.

The problem came at the third go-round, where Stevie Ray Vaughan had tossed in two extra beats. Jimmy, having heard the song a thousand times, was going by feel when he should have been counting like the rest of them.

"Try it this way," said Bobby. He played the riff then counted, "Five six seven eight one-and..."

Jimmy looked confused.

"No-no," Shawn said. Just play to the break and count five beats from there. NA-na-NA, na-NAAA, na-na-na NA-na-NA — one two three four five NA NA NA na-NA-na-NA..."

Jimmy squeezed his forehead. "Brain... hurts!"

"It's getting late," said Ivy. "Let's leave this till next time and let Jimmy listen to the tape."

"Yes!" Jimmy said.

Shawn was undoing the wing nut on his crash cymbal when Pancho came up, wearing a do-rag that made him look like a biker.

"Hey Shawn. That Guinness pretty good?"

"When I'm drumming, I drink nothing else. The Irish are a rhythmic people."

"Any left?"

"Sure. In the fridge. Just be sure to pour it in a glass right away. It's got this little nitrogen activator that makes it fizz up."

"Activator?"

"It's like the ball bearing in a can of spray paint."

"Oh. Okay. Thanks."

Next was Ivy, winding a microphone cord around her arm.

"Hey Shawn. Did you ask about the studio?"

"Yeah. We're all set. All we need is some decor. I'll handle the cleaning and painting, but I'll need you guys to bring some furnishings: a rug, some chairs, posters."

"Wednesday okay?"

"Oh. I didn't tell you – I can't do Wednesdays anymore."

"Girlfriend?"

"Yes."

"Nasty, dirty sex?"

"If you mean that in a good way, yes."

"Sorry. Living vicariously. What if we just show up an hour early on Thursday?"

"Groovy. What is that noise?"

"Metal sorta clicking noise?"

"Yeah."

They went to the kitchen, where Pancho was shaking his Guinness like a can of spray paint.

Shawn didn't know what to expect from Richard's studio. So much more the surprise when Shelly opened the door to a blank white room with beige industrial carpets and a row of empty cabinets. The only oddity was a water stain next to a door that had been nailed shut. He surmised that Richard must have rigged a hose through the door for his "cooking."

"By the way," said Shelly. "I'm still paying you."

"No way!" said Shawn.

Shelly put a hand to his forearm. "Awful lot of bad karma, Shawn."

"I'll use primer."

She fixed him with her eyes. "It'll take more than paint. It's going to take hours and hours of music. So please, let me pay you."

Shawn smiled. "I'm just poor enough to say yes."

"Oh, and one more thing."

"Mm-hmm?"

"Go nuts. Colors that you would never recommend to anyone. And make them work. But for now, you're on your own, 'cause this place is giving me the creeps."

With such demanding deadlines – musical and decorative – Shawn was grateful for the new arrangement with Tacoma. He missed her, though, and found himself audibly sighing as he worked. He had never believed that lovers actually did such things, had always dismissed them as Shakespearean exaggerations.

He painted the walls in a precarious lemon yellow, the mouldings, trim and cabinets in a lime green called Yucca Spring. Then he took a bright terra cotta to the front door, and the round wooden knobs of the cabinets.

He unscrewed one of the knobs, dipped it into the terra cotta and stamped circles along the tops of the walls. Using generous amounts and making three circles for each dipping, he guaranteed that each of his creatures would display a unique set of drips and flaws.

"Wow! Shawn! Lemon-lime! Dude!"

Ivy entered with four exclamations and a cardboard tube.

"Here. We need to figure out our territories and mark them

accordingly."

Shawn extracted the posters and immediately claimed one.

"Gene Krupa! Righteous!"

Ivy let out a shopper's grin. "I knew you'd like it. You'll also find Stevie Ray in a fringed sombrero..."

"Jimmy," said Shawn.

"An old sepia-tone Robert Johnson..."

"Pancho."

"Charlie Mingus in a smoke-filled room..."

"Bobby. And for Ivy, I'm guessing... Janis Joplin?"

"Not even close!"

"Ah," Shawn said, unrolling a young Ella Fitzgerald. "Excellent choice."

Pancho showed up with an old Persian rug, Jimmy with a rag-tag loveseat. Bobby brought beer. Shawn sat at his drums for half an hour as the guitarists tuned up and discussed obscure new devices for distorting sound. At the first second of silence they all looked at each other.

"Okay," said Jimmy. "I have applied actual numbers to the Stevie Ray Conundrum, and I think I've got it. Count us off, Shawn?"

Moss Green

Shawn realized his knowledge of C.S. Lewis came completely from some Anthony Hopkins and Debra Winger movie. Armed with such limited information, he was a third of the way through *The Lion, the Witch and the Wardrobe* before he realized it was a direct allegory for the gospel. Witness the lion who gives up his life so the two children might live. Subtle as a fart.

Or a knock on the door.

"Shawn! I realize it's a guy thing, but do you think I could get in there before noon?"

"Apologies, darling one! I'm caught up in your book."

"Haven't your butt-cheeks fallen asleep?"

"The lion just bought the farm!"

"Oh," she said. "That part is so sad. But I still have to pee!"

"Just a sec!"

Shawn washed his hands, then turned to the title page and read his favorite part.

> *To my dearest, darling Shawn. May you be the C.S. Lewis of drummers, and may you have every last thing you want (especially me!). Hugs, kisses, rrowr-rrowr! and most of all love.*
> *– Tacoma Davenport*

Funny how she always signed her last name like that. Like he might confuse her with all the other girls named Tacoma. He met her halfway down the hall, where he grabbed her by the waist and deposited kisses on her neck.

"If you keep doing that, I'll never get to the shower."

"I like you dirty."

Tacoma pulled back and said, "What do you mean by that?"

"Nothing. Trying to be clever. Want an omelet?"

"Umm, sure. Bell peppers and 'shrooms are in the fridge. And Swiss. Only, hold it fifteen minutes, wouldja? I'm going to soak a little."

"Sure."

Shawn was watching a documentary on jazz when she reappeared, wearing an odd ensemble: Birkenstock sandals with white woolen socks, tattered burgundy corduroys and a University of Washington sweatshirt.

"Laundry day," she said. "You wears what you gots."

"Would you like that omelet now?" he asked.

"You know, honey? It's very sweet of you, but I'm not really hungry and I need to hurry so I can get down to the office for a couple hours. So, no offense, but could you... skedaddle?"

"Oh," said Shawn. "Sure. We've got a sound check at two, so — yeah."

He fetched his jacket and headed down the steps, pivoting on the porch to let the five-inch differential bring their eyes level. He was met with a question.

"Are you all right, Shawn? Are we all right?"

His instinct was to laugh, but he saw that she was being serious.

"I think about you constantly. I'm happier than I have ever been."

She traced a finger along his collarbone. "You seem distracted. Sometimes I say things and you don't hear me."

He kissed her on the cheek. "I'm a guy. And this gig tonight... I'll try harder."

She gave him a look that seemed oddly blank. Then snapped it away like a bad hat.

"Yes. Of course. And don't worry — you'll be great. I don't know. Maybe I'm just being a chick."

"That's allowed. Seven o'clock? My place?"

She smiled. "See you soon, Bubba."

She lent him a pillowy kiss and waved as he turned the corner. Shawn's attentions turned deftly to the day's agenda: to Sluggo's for new sticks, Shakabrah for the sound check, figure out what to wear, grab a nap. He flipped C.S. Lewis onto the passenger seat and rolled down the window.

Black. A blues drummer should always wear black. And layers, because the spots would heat up and he'd have to strip down. Black tee, black jeans, black button-down. He tried on a black fedora and had immediate visions of cheese. Nuh-uh.

The fashion process had him running a little late, but he wasn't worried. They'd run such a thorough sound check that they'd be able to hop on stage and literally be playing in five seconds. But Tacoma was late, too — fifteen minutes. That wasn't like her. The intercom let out a scream.

"Joe's Pizza."

The joke flew right past her. "Pardon?"

"Stay there. I'll be right down."

Entering the lobby, Shawn could see that something was wrong. She was wearing the same clothes: Birkenstocks, corduroys, UW sweatshirt. And no makeup, which for Tacoma was unheard-of. He leaned through the door.

"Did you want to... come in?"

She gave him a blank look. "Why?"

"I thought you might want to... freshen up."

"What for?"

His boyfriend alarm-bells were going off full-blast. It almost seemed like she was looking to pick a fight.

"Nothing," he said. "All right if we take your car?"

He swung through the door and went to kiss her, but she jerked back as if he had just spit on her.

Oh man, he thought. *This is bad.* He ran through the past few days, looking for some small crime he may have committed. She turned to go, then stopped to look at him again, as if horns had just sprouted from his head.

"Let's go," she said. He followed her to the car, and accepted the keys when she asked him to drive. He was about to crank the ignition when she put a hand on his elbow.

"Wait, Shawn. I think you're in trouble, and I have something that could help you. I think we need to talk about Jesus."

She reached under the passenger seat, pulled out a large Bible, and began flipping through the pages.

"I think there's a passage in Corinthians..."

There it was, the rejection, the big lie. Despite everything she knew about him, here it was, some crazy attempt at a foxhole conversion. The muscles in his abdomen drew tight.

"Stop," he said. He made his decision quickly. "I have to go."

He got out and walked, afraid to look back. He went up to his apartment and sat by the window, in darkness. Five minutes later, she drove away.

He found himself watching the American flag atop City Hall. Then, his alarm clock went off. No, it was the phone. He waited for the caller to leave a message.

"Shawn? Where the hell are you?" It was Ivy. "We're getting worried, sonnyboy. We're on in half an hour. Give me a call at..."

"Hi. Ivy? Sorry, I was screening. Listen..."

"Are you okay? You sound weird."

"Um... upset," said Shawn. He proceeded to the mathematics at hand: *What will it take to get me through this?*

"Listen, Ivy. I'll tell you about it after. I'll probably need to. But for now, just pretend everything's normal, okay? Trouble with my battery. Left my lights on."

"Sure, Shawn. Are you okay to drive?"

"Yeah. I'll be there in ten minutes. And forget about me, okay? Enjoy your singing, and kick some ass up there. It's nothing life-and-death, just..."

"Girlfriend?"

"Yeah. Girlfriend."

Shawn was able to shut himself down when needed. When he was sixteen, a friend was killed in a boating accident. Another boat rammed into theirs late at night. His friend was decapitated. Too shaken to speak for themselves, the family asked Shawn to deliver the eulogy.

At the service, Shawn felt himself elevated, sealed off. His friend had been blessed with a large heart and quick wit, and Shawn was determined to get this across. He told a handful of small, funny stories, spoke so calmly he was on the verge of seeming cold-blooded, detached. But people laughed, and smiled, and that was what he wanted. Five hours later, driving to the store to pick up some groceries for his mom, Shawn heard his friend's favorite song on the radio. He pulled off the road and sobbed for half an hour.

So here he was, another assignment, another levee around his heart. After a single mother-bear look of concern, Ivy did him the great favor of keeping him busy, handing him a set list and running through some last-minute changes.

After that, the night was a blur. He remembered Jimmy going into a raging guitar solo on "Stormy Monday," playing with his teeth, and behind his head. The band wasn't entirely sure if he intended to stop. And all along, Shawn was building up the volume, starting with brushes, then flipping around to the handles. By the time Jimmy nodded the final turn, Shawn was whanging the cymbals full-tilt, one-two-three-four, one-two... He hit the cut on his hi-hat and then stomped it, sucking sound from the air. The audience had no choice but to scream their heads off. They had no idea how deftly their buttons had been pushed.

Ivy was on her game too, shaking and growling, pulling back for a sugary turn of phrase. Shawn thought how much of the blues was theater, how thoroughly you had to invest yourself in a character. Halfway through the second set, the usually listless Shakabrah crowd got up and danced, staying there through the finale — "They Raided the Joint." Shawn's drum break was a gem of small geometries, punching into the spaces, working the toms till they demanded a cymbal, and then the snare, ending with spitfire rolls to the crash. If drumming were Zen, perhaps it was best to ruin one's life right before a gig. Shawn's mind contained nothing but fuzz, and he appeared to be playing beautifully.

"Ivy and the Swingin' Richards!"

Somebody shouted their name into a mic and the crowd let loose a volley of hoots and applause. A minute later, as the whoops dwindled to a drunken few, Shawn slipped out the back and threw up in the alley.

Whoever designed the Tacoma Narrows Bridge, hated pedestrians.

Tightroping the three-foot walkway, Shawn felt the thrust as each car came close to blowing him to smithereens.

People knew the Narrows, whether they thought they did or not. Its predecessor, known by the locals as Gallopin' Gertie, swung herself to pieces in the channel's high winds. Her death throes, caught on film by a local photographer, had since become a staple of disaster documentaries.

Shawn was betting on Gertie II being a little steadier, though it hardly mattered — a midnight overcast was holding the wind to five knots. Nearing the first of the bridge's two towers, Shawn felt the call of completion. He knew he wouldn't be happy unless he walked all the way across. It would also give him time to think. Some kid leaned out the window of a passing car and yelled either "Jump!" or "Don't jump!" Neither of which helped.

Thank God for Ivy. At a time when she really should have been collecting plaudits on the coffeehouse floor, she chose to spend 45 minutes in a vomit-smelling alley with her heartbroken drummer. As a do-it-yourself pagan, and a lover of natural cycles, Ivy had always expected Tacoma to "go Billy Graham" on his ass. To her credit, she stayed away from the obvious Christian-bashing, choosing instead to offer gentle questions and vague consolations. And made him promise to drive straight home, and not to do anything foolish.

Was this foolish? Probably. He watched his steps eat up the span until he found himself over the edge of the Kitsap Peninsula. He tapped the end of the railing and turned back.

His new adversaries were blinding headlights and kicked-up dust — but the moon was out, three-quarters, slipping through cottage-cheese curds of cloud. The waters below were dark and sleek, offering up riptide lagoons of light. The city showed very little of itself, swales of suburbia dripping over the bluffs like cake frosting.

He found a couple walking toward him, a slim blue-jeaned boy in a funky bowl haircut, a jet-haired girl with twin ponytails, dressed in a retro satin skirt. Considering the setting, Shawn prepared a reassuring greeting.

"Glad to see I'm not the only one."

The girl laughed shyly, and they walked on toward Gig Harbor.

Was this their idea of a romantic date? Will he kiss her halfway across?

Not if they followed the "No Standing" signs posted every 200 feet, halfway between the emergency call boxes. The bridge was trouble.

He settled on a stripe of dark near the Tacoma-side tower and peered upward, a blocky moss-green shoot stitched with rivets. Suitably impressed, he leaned over the railing, the water too dark to inspire vertigo, and set to his business.

The pages ripped away easily, but Shawn took his time, offering each its own little death. Together, they formed a smoke-like trail of white leaves, striking the water in a slow drift toward the Pacific.

Take that, you proselytizing bastard.

Perhaps it didn't help at all, sending C.S. Lewis to a watery grave, but Shawn felt better for doing something so foolish and picturesque. He spotted a pair of plastic bouquets, strapped to the railings in remembrance of suicides past, then discovered he had to drive all the way across the bridge before turning around.

He couldn't resist the quick bypass to Tacoma's house, and was surprised when he didn't see her car. *Out fucking some Baptist,* he thought, enjoying his viciousness. He found his immediate reward in a vivid mental image, the two of them boinking atop the altar in some dark sanctuary.

God, this really sucks.

Arriving home, he tortured himself further, imagining Tacoma with men of all faiths and penis sizes – Hindus with foreskins, Muslims with twelve-inchers – wasting all that brilliant lovemaking on true believers when it was he, Shawn, who believed in *her*. He fell into a fitful sleep, convinced that he was on his own again — the way he had planned it, the morning he left Ellensburg.

Butterscotch

That wasn't Tacoma.

Three words arrived with the sun. Shawn stumbled to his desk and punched in the numbers. He got her answering machine.

He had her roommate's number somewhere, for emergencies. He dug through his drawers, and then remembered the card was in his wallet, the numbers in Tacoma's big, looping cursive. His call was answered by a bleary female voice.

"Mmello?"

"Hi. Is this... Suzanne?"

"If you want it to be. Is this Shawn?"

The quick recognition surprised him. She traveled a lot — he'd only met her once.

"She's at the hospital."

"Huh?"

"Tacoma. The hospital. I had to call the cops to take her in. Not that she was dangerous, but when she gets into one of these Jesus things, she's..."

"Wait a minute. Jesus things?"

"Yeah. She gets hyper-religious. She won't eat, says, 'Jesus will be my food.' Drives through red lights 'cause Jesus will take care of her. Last time she said it was some guy in Seattle, sold her some bad tea. I had to stay up with her half the night just to get her through it. I'm glad they took her in this time. She really needs to have it checked out. When was the last time you saw her? Shawn?"

"Oh. Sorry. This is a little... weird. Where did you say they took her?"

"Not really sure. Some sort of mental emergency ward. They gave me a number, though."

Shawn wrote it down and thanked Suzanne for handling things. He hung up, and the tiles clicked into place: the Seattle episode, Tacoma's phobia about the occult, last night's bizarre behavior. It seemed selfish to think so, but he was relieved to know it had not been a rejection after all, that perhaps they still had a future together. And that he had something simple and serious to focus on.

He called the number and got a woman with a slight Nordic accent, as if all her vowels had umlauts.

"No, I'm afraid you won't be able to see her for a couple of days. We're keeping her under sedation until the doctors can get a clear diagnosis. Why don't I give you the number for the release clinic in Steilacoom? She's a pretty mild case, so they'll probably send her there tomorrow. Call this number Tuesday morning, and they'll tell you what to do next."

The next two days were sheer hell. He had no idea what she was going through, if she understood that her brain had betrayed her. Fortunately, he had work. Shelly was doing her upstairs library in butterscotch yellow, with the same blood red for trim. Shawn spent the morning lugging books into the hall, enjoying the rigor, the strain and stretch of his muscles.

Shelly's arthritis was acting up, so instead of making sandwiches she treated him to lunch at The Spar, a bricky lunchplace in the Old Town district. They stayed for two hours, resembling a man and his grandmother out for a visit, as Shawn recounted his mystifying weekend.

After lunch, he called the clinic, and was informed that he could come by at seven the next evening.

Steilacoom lay south of Tacoma, a comfy town centered on a waterfront green and a ferry dock. Shawn was surprised that such a place would allow a mental health clinic, but he could see how they snuck it under the radar. It sat two blocks up from the water, three modest brick buildings identified only as Steilacoom Acres. It wouldn't surprise him if tourists occasionally stopped in to ask about a room.

Shawn slipped cautiously through the twin glass doors of the office and approached a large black woman seated expectantly behind the reception desk.

"Hi. Um... I'm here to see..."

She did have a way of making an entrance: at the end of the hallway, wrapped in a white bathrobe, her face scrubbed clean, her hair hanging to either side in damp ringlets. She gave him a resigned smile, worn down by life and medication, but having spotted the light at the end of her tunnel. The light walked her way in firm strides, recording every inch of her, the most beautiful vision he had ever encountered.

Sky Blue

Two large white creatures are standing on an iceberg. One of them says, "I don't know — I'm up, I'm down, I'm up again. My doctor says I'm a bipolar bear."

That was the joke he told Tacoma when the meds and the cautious lifestyle started getting to her. Now, it was the first thing he thought of when he woke up, every morning.

"Shawn! Hey Shawn!"

That and the guys yelling outside. Their friend's intercom didn't work, so they shouted four stories' worth, at all times of day or night, until their friend dropped his keys out the window.

"Shawn! Yo buddy!"

And fate would have it that they shared a name. Shawn peered through the blinds, in case he had to identify them in a police lineup. A set of keys whipped past the Washington flag, just missing George's nose. But Shawn no longer cared — there was life at the Kickstand Café.

The Kickstand had been under construction for months, its windows covered by butcher paper. A sign on the door announced the grand opening, but every two weeks the date was pushed back.

Lord knows, Shawn needed a reprieve. The Christian café was pulling out the big guns. First they went to 24 hours, seven days a week. Then they brought in a crowd of beautiful young women from a Russian Orthodox church. They would sit around in tight dresses and leather jackets, chatting in their native tongue. Shawn started drinking iced mochas.

But now, the butcher paper was gone, and there were fresh lattes a mere hundred feet from his window! He was so excited, he forgot to shave. He stood at the entrance, running a hand over his stubble as he sized up the decor.

The interior had walls of scrubbed raw sienna, like a trendy Italian restaurant. The left and right windows offered blonde-wood counters fixed by exposed chromium bolts. The front counter cruised by like a small art-deco boat, wearing a crescent of silvery faux-marble. The back wall was capped by a crown of steel plate, spars of copper jutting upward like sun-rays.

Standing behind a man in a tall white cowboy hat, Shawn caught a glimpse of the counter girl, who was terribly typecast: several earrings, hoop over one eyebrow, and a stripe of sky-blue hair. The cowboy took his cappuccino and scooted left. Shawn's pupils grew several sizes.

"Wendy?"

He returned when she got off work, and drove them to the end of Ruston Way. He walked her to his favorite bench, looking over the water to Vashon Island. He liked to sit here in the evening and imagine that the Puget Sound was his own cozy neighborhood, the houselights of the island coming on one at a time like evening stars. On sunny afternoons, you could look to the east, where a trick of depth perception made it look like the high-rise apartments were just across the street from Mt. Rainier.

Today, Tahoma was hiding her head under a blanket of smoky overcast. Wendy held her jacket collar to her neck, releasing a shy smile that seemed to make all the piercings disappear.

"God, Shawn. All those years of you trying to corrupt me. I should have let you! I was very well-trained, you know. My mom and all that shit about buying the cow. Did it ever occur to her that the cow *likes* being milked?"

All this sudden hedonism was hitting Shawn right in the funny bone. He envisioned a Holstein in a pink negligee and burst out laughing.

"What?" asked Wendy.

"Hard to explain," said Shawn, catching his breath. "Cows are naturally funny. Ducks, too. So how the hell did you end up a hundred feet from my apartment?"

"My cool cousin Laurel. She was working for an alternative weekly in Olympia and got tired of the slave wages, decided to open a café with her boyfriend. She came for a visit last month, about the same time I was picking all those meaningless fights with my parents. It's hell being a preacher's daughter, especially when you realize you don't believe a fucking word of it. I figured if I was going to publicly go to hell, I should at least leave the county. Probably broke my parents' hearts, but they have no idea how lucky they are."

"So basically," said Shawn. "You wore my poor agnostic prick to the nub, and all the while you were a closet heathen yourself?"

"I was trying so hard to believe, but the constant contradictions finally got to me. Hell, just look at the trial. Any idiot knows that the Romans would off a political dissident at the drop of a hat. They certainly wouldn't put it to a vote of whatever Jews happened to be in court that day! But wouldn't Paul and his copywriters be brilliant marketers if they managed to blame the crucifixion, seventy years after the fact, on the very group that was most staunchly boycotting their new product? And simultaneously exonerate the Romans, who turned out to be their most lucrative target audience?"

"You, young lady, are Jimmy Swaggart's worst nightmare."

"So what about you? Are you doing okay out here?"

"Yeah. I'm playing in a blues band that is actually planning a tour..."

"Wow!"

"I have a nice day job painting a house that never ends and... well... I've got a nice apartment."

"Wait," she said. "Go back. Fill in that empty space where you were going to mention the girl."

Shawn laughed. "God, you're good. Okay. Her name was Tacoma. Flaming bumper-sticker Christian girl."

"Jesus! Did you not learn your lesson?"

"No. And it wouldn't matter if I did. Might as well tell a meteor not to give in to the Earth's gravity."

She gazed at him with a wide grin.

"What?"

"Poetry," she said. "You loved her, didn't you?"

"Yeah."

"So why all the past tense?"

Shawn wrapped a knee with his fingers.

"Tough question. But I've got a theory. I think a successful relationship needs a few months when everything's easy. That way, when you run into the bad spots, later on, you can reach back to that period as a kind of touchstone. Two months after we met, Tacoma went nuts."

"But every woman's entitled to an occas..."

"No-no," said Shawn. "I mean that literally. She had an episode, she was taken to a mental health clinic, and diagnosed with bipolar syndrome. Her mom's got it, too. The weird thing was, it only served to intensify my feelings. I wanted to battle the beast right alongside her.

"A few weeks later, when she was beginning to adjust, I told her I loved her. I said it whenever I saw her, simply because it was true, and I enjoyed saying it. I don't think she believed me. I still haven't figured it out, but I'm betting it goes back to her childhood. She was pretty much tossed around like a beach ball. It's amazing she turned out as well as she did. But I think she associates the phrase 'I love you' with 'I'll be leaving you now.'"

"So, do you think she loved you?"

"She managed to say it a few times. But I knew, regardless. Just about everything she did..."

Wendy gazed out toward Vashon, where a container ship was making its way to the Tacoma port. She worried that she was prying, but she couldn't stop.

"Tell me how it ended."

"A friend of mine hooked us up with a yacht race in Bremerton. Not a speed race. They cover up all the clocks and try to hit certain spots at certain times, using only speed, wind and current. Tacoma and I were serving as monitors. They'd pass a certain landmark and yell out 'Mark!' and we would write down the time. In return, we got a free lunch, free drinks and a trip on some rich guy's yacht."

"Sign me up!" said Wendy.

"I don't know if they'd go for the blue hair."

"I'll wear a hat."

"So where was I?"

"Puget Sound."

"Right. So there we are, chugging past Blake Island... Seattle skyline... brilliant May morning, chill wind ruffling our hair. We should be having the time of our lives, but instead we're just miserable. Tacoma has had it with me loving her so much, and I'm tired of beating my head against a wall. Later, I'm driving us home, past that little bay at Port Orchard, and I look at Tacoma snoozing in the passenger seat, and I realize... we're all done. She woke up when we turned onto Sixth Street, and we conducted our final negotiations on the way to her house. I haven't seen her in two months."

Wendy felt bad that she had taken Shawn down this path, and decided to make up for it.

"So. Would you like to go somewhere and fuck?"

That did make him feel better. At least, the thought of it.

"I don't know. Why don't you give me one of those Tonight Show kisses?"

Wendy straddled him on the bench, settling against his lap with a familiar belly-dancer twist, and delivered a fat showbiz smooch. When she came up for air, she could read her failure at a glance.

"Wow. Bummer."

She sprawled on the bench, one hand still hooked around his neck.

Shawn chuckled. "My lead guitarist is kinda cute."

"Oh, thanks a lot!"

Blonde

Tacoma's job, and her medical need for stable hours, had put an end to their excursions. Now, with Wendy in town, Shawn was able to start anew. They took the long 101 loop around the Olympic Mountains, stopping at the Hoh Rain Forest to check out the moss-covered trees. Further along the coast, they walked groves of spruce pregnant with burls, and watched curtains of steam ghosting the dirt-brown beaches. After that it was Cape Flattery, the meeting-point of Tacoma's ill-fated parents. Walking a trail of logs to the observation deck, they found slate-gray cliffs, a cove with several shades of blue-green water, and rugged seastacks topped with evergreens. A bald eagle split the air with his gestureless flight, his head a shocking white.

"Jesus!" Wendy whispered. "It's a fucking Spielberg film."

Wendy's initial lap-dance turned out to be a blessing, illustrating how much he was still stuck on Tacoma, and freeing him up to enjoy Wendy's pagan rebirth on a lust-free level. It occurred to him that her former prickteasings had produced exactly the opposite of their intended effect. He was so obsessed about getting into her pants that he never got to know her as a person.

Ivy began their next rehearsal with the news that they had finally gotten a gig at Cole's. The club wasn't much to look at – it was small and a little bit seedy – but Cole's was where all the real blues bands played, so getting in was quite a score. Ivy also reported that her trombonist daddy knew a winner when he heard one, and was putting up the bucks for a demo CD.

Getting home from all this great news, Shawn was much too wired to sleep. He put on a Count Basie record and prepared to do some weightlifting. And he thought about Angie.

If L.A. were the City of Angels, Tacoma was the City of Angies: Jimmy Catarino's girlfriend, Wendy's coworker, the manager at Shakabrah – there were Angies everywhere. Shawn's Angie lived in a basement apartment across from the laundry room. He was headed there with an armful of dirty clothes when he spotted her in the hall, complaining to the manager, Andrew, about fourth-floor Sean and his bellowing friends.

"Half the time, when he throws his keys down there, they land in the bushes, and then I've got these creeps digging around outside my window."

Shawn was glad to join in, motivated mostly by Angie's long blonde hair and cutesy Sally Struthers appearance.

Now, midway through his wrist curls, Shawn heard a loud crash on the street. He looked outside to see a wheel rolling down the middle of Sixth Avenue. Expecting some great NASCAR pileup, he peered up the street but found nothing. It wasn't until he tiptoed outside in bare feet that he found the cause: a blue sedan, chips of glass scattered around its rear end like autumn leaves.

Shawn called the police, and then stood watch at the window as a patrol car pulled up. A tall, balding officer got out to inspect the scene. Two minutes later, Shawn's phone rang.

"Hello, Mister Turk? This is the Tacoma Police calling back? Could you do us a favor? We have the resident manager listed in Apartment 108 — name of Angela? Could you pop down there and wake her? We don't want to alarm her — but we do need to find out who owns the car."

Shawn was happy to help out, but realized halfway down the

elevator that Angie wasn't the manager — Andrew was. He knocked anyway, figuring something would come out in the wash.

"Hello? Who is it?"

"Hi," he said, uncertainly. "It's Shawn — from 308? There's a car that's been broken into... and they asked me to wake you."

The door didn't open, but the voice got grumpier. "At one-thirty in the morning? And I'm not the manager. Why did they... Oh God." She cracked open the door. "It's not a Honda, is it? I just got that car."

"I'm not sure," said Shawn. "I thought it was a BMW. I'm sorry, they must have made a mistake. I'll go check with the officer."

Angie grunted and closed the door.

Excuse me for being a good citizen, thought Shawn. Still, heading outside, he thought how cute she looked in her flowered PJs. By the time he got close enough to see the "H" on the car's grille, Angie was walking down the front steps in bathrobe and slippers.

"Oh God! Oh shit..."

That was about the extent of her outburst. Shawn had to admire her composure. She sat in the patrol car, answering questions for the report as Shawn stood on the sidewalk, chatting with the tall, balding officer.

"Are you the one who called?" he asked.

"Yeah, that's me."

"Thanks for doing that. Woulda been a shame to leave it out here like this."

"Were they trying to steal something?" Shawn asked.

"Nope. Strictly for funzies."

"They used a tire, right?"

"Yep." The officer pointed downhill to the Walker Apartments. "Came to a stop under those trees."

"Oh, good," said Shawn. "For a second, I thought I was

hallucinating."

"Pretty common trick. Old wheel makes a good smashing device. So, are you familiar with fourth-floor Sean?"

"God, yes! And all his frickin-frackin friends, too."

"He's up there right now, scoping us out."

Shawn turned to see a thin silhouette in the apartment above his.

"Claims he used to work for the FBI," said the cop, shaking his head. "Piece of work, that one."

"Hope he gets a goddamn intercom someday."

"I hear they're taking care of it tomorrow."

"Shawn! Yo, Shawn!"

"Oh, sorry" said Shawn. "This one's for me."

He hiked across the street, where Wendy was standing with a large figure who turned out to be his guitarist, Pancho. *Guy moves fast*, he thought. He had only told him about Wendy that night.

"Pancho! What's it been? Four hours?"

"Five, at most," Pancho said with a grin. "Went to grab a post-rehearsal java, and I met your buddy here."

"We were shooting pool across the street," said Wendy. "Your friend here's a real crack shot."

"I-i-i'm gonna walk away from that straight line," said Shawn.

"So what's the excitement?" asked Pancho.

"Cute blonde downstairs got her car window bashed in. I'm the lucky sap who got to wake her up."

"I know you've been lonely, pal, but that's going just a little bit too far." Pancho's eyes cut past Shawn's shoulder. Angie was crossing the street to join them.

"Hi," she said. "I want to thank you for going to all the trouble. I'm sorry I was such a bitch."

"Understandable," said Shawn. "Seems like you've had a traumatic week."

"It's been… challenging." She sighed and bit her lip in a way that made Shawn's blood rise.

"Hey," said Pancho. "Seeing as no one here is getting any sleep tonight, why don'tch'all come to my house for spaghetti?"

"Pancho's quite a cook," said Wendy. "Or so he tells me."

"I'd like to," said Angie. "But I have to wait for the tow truck."

"I'll wait with you," said Shawn. "You guys go ahead. We'll be there soon."

"Well then," Angie said with a smile, "I guess I'd better get out of these PJs."

"I got no problem with your PJs," said Shawn. *Wow*, he thought. *I'm flirting with a woman-not-Tacoma.*

Angie smiled. "I'll put on some jeans."

Angie was quiet all the way over — probably, thought Shawn, ruminating on her lousy luck. She seemed to perk up as they neared Pancho's apartment, across the street from the baseball stadium. They entered to the smells of garlic and cooked meat. Pancho and Wendy sat among dirty dishes, playing some sort of card game.

"Got any twos?" said Pancho.

"Go fuck yourself," said Wendy. "How about… jacks?"

"Go fuck yourself," said Pancho.

Shawn peered over Pancho's shoulder. "This can't be what I think it is."

"Yeah – Go Fish," said Wendy, straight-faced.

"And when you win," said Pancho, "you say 'Hoosier Daddy!' Which, of course, refers to Les Newport, a father of seven from

Greenfield, Indiana. What about nines?"

"Go fuck yourself," said Wendy.

"Damn!" Pancho scowled and took a card from the pile. "Plates and pasta is in the kitchen, guys. And grab those last two garlic breads before I do."

"He really is a good cook," said Wendy, flashing Shawn a secret smile.

Shawn and Angie ate voraciously, and then lit up cigarettes, though neither was a smoker. They tried out the new game, and Shawn was pleased at Angie's fondness for the f-word. He didn't trust women who didn't cuss.

He found pleasures, too, in the hubbub of their party: Pancho's rumbling voice, Wendy's occasional squeals, the click and smack of playing cards. *Look at me*, he thought. *I've got a circle of friends.*

His meditation was interrupted by Angie, who smiled wickedly and slammed her cards to the table.

"Hoosier Daddy, Bitch!"

Shawn laughed. "You are. And by the way, if you're still wired after this, I know a great all-night coffeehouse."

Apple Cider

Whatever happened with Angie would take a while. She and Shawn both seemed more comfortable quartetting it with Wendy and Pancho. When they were alone, they both seemed distracted and inert. Occasionally, their eyes would flash in conversation, or he would make her laugh. He loved her sharp wit, her jaded outlook, but for whatever reason the loop refused to close.

They began to fall into the habits of friendship: going Dutch, the goodnight hug. It might have been simple chemistry. After Tacoma, Shawn knew the color of those sparks, and he wasn't getting that from Angie.

When they ran out of art films at the Grand, they gave into mass marketing and saw a Jackie Chan movie. Shawn hated to admit it, but the guy had turned martial arts into something new, half Baryshnikov, half Buster Keaton.

They pulled up to the Cambridge to find lawn furniture: a mattress, bookcase, kitchen table and three chairs. A flyer from the police department declared that these were the results of an eviction, and were not to be disturbed.

Shawn left Angie with their customary embrace and nearly skipped the two flights to his apartment. Fourth-floor Sean was history! He was still winded when he hit the answering machine and heard an unexpected voice.

"Hi Shawn. I hate to call just to take advantage of your muscle, but... I'm moving, and I really need some help. Could you rescue a lady in distress? Give me a call. Please."

Suzanne had been transferred out-of-state, leaving Tacoma with the choice of finding another roommate or another situation. She opted for a one-bedroom in a nice complex near Point Defiance. Its only drawback was a narrow staircase with a sharp right turn, making furniture navigation a particular pain. It didn't help that Tacoma kept cracking jokes at critical lifting moments, leaving Shawn somewhere between dying laughing and just plain dying.

The work was good, though, because it gave them a focus. They managed to avoid any awkwardness till later, consuming the requisite pizza as they scraped for things to say.

"How's the band?"

"Great! We're playing Cole's tomorrow night."

"Cole's! Isn't that the one you've been shooting for?"

"Yeah. The *real* blues joint. They don't let you play there unless you've been in jail at least once."

Oh, that did it. She smiled. He could fend off anything but that.

"Would you mind if I... showed up?" she asked.

Shawn smiled back. "I'd be honored."

The next day, Shawn's mind was a hundred miles away. He should have been relaxing, perhaps running some songs through his head. Instead, he was running Tacoma through his head, trying to figure if this reunion really meant something.

His answer came in a common term of male appraisal, uttered by Pancho as Shawn knelt on the stage, tuning his bass drum.

"Hachiwawa!"

She walked through the door in black leather go-go boots, chocolate suede miniskirt, black-and-gold sleeveless sequin top, and a jacket of black see-through lace extending to her wrists.

Artemis, thought Shawn. *The Huntress.* It was time to make some quick decisions.

Ivy had just told them about a festival in Twin Falls, Idaho. She wanted to line up clubs on the way there and back, and make a tour of it. For Shawn, it was a life's dream, and he wanted it all for himself. There were lots of tales about drummers and groupies, and he wanted to skim those shallow waters just once. So he coached himself: *Make no promises.*

He tightened the last head-nut and went to the bar, where Tacoma was sipping from a Roy Rogers. He ran a finger down the back of her neck and watched her apple-cider eyes as she turned.

"Hi."

"Hi. You look incredible."

"Y'look pretty good yourself."

"Nonsense. I look like a drummer. You look like a czarina."

After such pleasant beginnings, it was easy to fall into old habits. At the first break, he held her hand under the table. At the second, he opened her fingers and kissed her palm. She responded by kissing his jawline just under the earlobe.

Matters weren't helped by the band, which was operating like a beautiful machine. They knew the music well enough that they could swim around in it. Halfway through "I Just Want to Make Love to You," Shawn extended the drum break into a hip-hop beat, smacking those interior James Brown snare shots and refusing to cue the guitarists back in. Ivy jumped to the mic, taking an old sexuo-political poem ("Mister/Misses") and laying it out over the drum track.

Drinking a post-gig martini, unable to keep his facial features from rising, the loveliest girl on God's green planet on his arm, Shawn was an easy target. Tacoma whispered an invitation, and Shawn responded with a breath-stealing kiss, raising a round of hoots and hollers from the twelve people left in the bar.

Pink

Shawn's horseshoe stood on its toes, leaning against the stake like a drunk on a bar. Tacoma's cartwheeled in, hooked him by the collar and yanked him off his feet. He landed a foot away, flat on his back, staring at the cloud-spotted sky.

"You bitch!"

"Tee-hee."

"That was so rude!"

"There are no manners in horseshoes."

The day before the blues tour, they were walking through Wright Park when they stumbled on ten pair of horseshoe pits. Each end was fitted with a wooden rain shelter; one of them read, "Tacoma Horseshoe Club." Tacoma insisted that they go out and buy some shoes.

Two weeks after the tour, it was clear that one of them had been practicing. She had developed a low-trajectory toss that cleared out his point-makers like a linebacker taking out quarterbacks. His only chance was to fall behind on points, forcing her to throw first. Sadly, this was not hard to do.

Tacoma hurled the next one so low it barely cleared the grass. It landed on the dirt and slid straight ahead, embracing the stake with its outspread arms. Tacoma, 15 to 13.

"Aiee," cried Shawn, face in hands.

"Poor honey," Tacoma cooed. "Just remember what a nice winner I can be." She slapped him on the butt.

"I'll keep that in mind," Shawn said, collecting their shoes. "Would you like to whoop me again, or would you prefer a mocha?"

"Oooh!"

She was so fond of the beverage that he'd taken to calling her "Tamocha." It came in handy for getting out of unpleasant situations.

"How come you never get that look when you look at me?" he asked.

"If you covered yourself in chocolate and espresso, maybe I would."

"Okay. But not hot espresso."

"Piker."

They carried their horsehoes downhill to the Kickstand.

"What the hell happened to the rest of the horse?"

Shawn leaned over the counter to give Wendy a kiss on the cheek.

"How 'bout a couple mochas, quick as you can make 'em?"

"Sure! Hi Tacoma, how ya doin'?"

"Just kicked my boyfriend's ass."

"Good. He deserves it, leaving you alone to go on tour. This woman is gorgeous, Shawn! Were you gonna find anyone like her in Idaho?"

"No," said Shawn.

"Good answer," said Wendy.

Tacoma and Shawn sat and talked about Tacoma's job. She'd been promoted to sales, and was excited at the chance to make more money. A half-hour later, they ran into Angie at the elevator.

"Angie!" said Shawn. He wrapped her in a hug and lifted her off the ground.

"Hi Shawn. How are ya?"

"Angie, this is Tacoma. Tacoma, my pal Angie. She lives in the basement with the mole people."

"But the rent is cheap" she said. "So, you're the legendary Tacoma! I'm so glad to see you guys back together. It was so obvious Shawn was still stuck on you. But hey — I gotta split. Movie date with a girlfriend. Let's get together sometime for a card game."

"Aw, go fuck yourself," Shawn said.

Angie laughed and pushed her way out the door.

After their lovemaking, Shawn lay flat on his back, staring through the blinds. Tacoma played with his hair, separating a lock, studying it, then setting it aside. Shawn could feel questions coming to the surface like koi in a pond.

"It was a nice day today," she said.

"Mm-hmm."

"It's a shame I have to go home."

"Then stay."

"No. Don't want to stress out the bipolar bear."

Shawn rose to his knees and stared at her.

"What?" she asked.

"Before you burst a blood vessel," he said, "you'd better ask me that question."

Tacoma ran both hands through her hair. "Well..." She took a breath that hunched her shoulders. "You're very popular."

"Yes?"

"With girls. You have a lot of girl... friends."

Shawn was working hard to keep that fatal first response from his lips. Tacoma went on.

"The girl who used to dry-hump you during the Tonight Show is making our mochas. And Angie, whose eyes go off like flash bulbs when she sees you..."

Shawn sat back on his haunches and put a hand on her knee.

"First thought: comparing Wendy or Angie to you is like comparing

Puyallup to Paris. Second: nothing happened with either one."

"Because they never gave you the chance?"

"Wendy propositioned me after three hours. And Lord, does she owe me a few. But she's the past. She's Ellensburg."

"So you turning her down had nothing to do with me."

"At the time, you and I were not together. I was free to do what I wanted. But you have succeeded in setting the bar so high that I didn't want to come down."

Tacoma seemed to enjoy that response, but she fought to maintain her prosecutor's demeanor.

"But you are attracted to Angie."

"Yes. Angie is attractive. But again, two unattached people, and nothing happened."

"Because she didn't give you the chance."

"She didn't jump all over me, no. But think about it: four, five dates and I didn't even try to hold her hand. I'm not a dog, Tacoma. I don't operate on automatic. Romance is like a third person in the room. It has to enter of its own accord."

Tacoma's eyes flicked back and forth. "A third person."

He brought his face to hers and said, "A third person, made up of the things that pass between two people."

He kissed her on the forehead and stood.

"Would you like some water?"

"Yes," she said.

He filled a glass at the sink, relieved that he had passed the gauntlet. Her question drifted over his shoulder like a yellowjacket.

"So what about the tour?"

He handed her the glass.

"It went very well."

"What about the girls of Idaho?"

He didn't have a good response, so he didn't say anything. Tacoma took a swallow and opened her eyes.

"So you and I... were not exclusive."

He opened the blinds, Rainier glowing pink in the sunset. Perhaps it would blow up and save him the trouble.

"I didn't have faith in us," he said. "not yet. And I was living out a dream. I wanted it... unfettered. I'm sorry. I was trying not to make any promises."

"Did anything... happen?"

"No."

"Because the girls of Idaho... didn't give you the chance?"

He had to hold that one for a while.

"Yes."

A tear leaked from the corner of her eye. Another contribution to the third person. He would've done anything to take it back.

He woke up at six o'clock, to the sound of his phone.

"Hello?"

"Hi. I'm sorry for waking you, but I can't go to work without..."

She stopped.

"Tacoma? What is it?"

"Are we exclusive... now?"

"Yes."

"Thanks. Now go back to sleep."

"Consider it done."

He slumped into the pillow, cordless in hand.

Pumpkin

Shawn knelt on the pumpkin-orange carpet of Shelly's basement, eyeing a wall of freshly primed wood paneling. *Shelly must be crazy to think I can pull this off,* he thought. He stabbed his putty knife into a bucket of joint compound and smacked a glob on the wall.

He ran the blade once, twice, then an S-curve through the center, till he flattened it to a quarter inch. He was beginning to see the pattern: Italian restaurants, artful swoops and cuts like the flight of a bird. As in algebra, the idea was to show the work. No room for straight lines or symmetrical intentions. In a blur of three hours, the wall was covered. Shawn sprawled on the carpet to stare, in love with his own work.

"Shawn, it looks fabulous! I knew you had the knack. Let's take lunch."

They went to Harbor Lights, a seafood place on Ruston Way. The sparkly lightbulbs of the sign reminded him of a Mafia hangout. Shelly signaled her intention to spend lots of money by ordering lobster. Shawn went for the swordfish.

"The man at the store said it would take twenty-four hours to dry, so I thought we should call it a day and eat someplace fancy."

"Sure," said Shawn. He tried not to think about his splattered jeans.

"So how are things with Tacoma?"

"Superb. I've never been this... deep before."

"That's wonderful, Shawn. She really is a beautiful girl. Tell me about her family."

"Her family?"

"Yeah. Let me play amateur psychologist."

"Okay. Well, Mom has bipolar, too. Dangerously chatty. Get her on the phone and she'll talk half an hour before you say hello. She seems to adore me, but I don't see how she could know."

"What about Dad?"

"Largely absent, after the divorce. But they're back in touch now. Lives in Gloucester, Massachusetts, where he does some sort of job in between fishing trips."

"So all this adds up to being raised by Grandma?"

"Yeah. Mom was pretty unstable. So she lived with Grandma in South Hills Pittsburgh. Grandma had lots of money — inheritance, I think. Had a live-in boyfriend, young black dancer, twenty years her junior."

Shelly laughed. "Grandma had style, didn't she?"

"Grandma was a babe. Vaudeville showgirl. Could've been in Ziegfield's Follies, but — well, long story. By the time Tacoma returned from college, Grandma had ditched the boyfriend and refocused her energies on running every five minutes of Tacoma's life. That's when she took off."

"God! It's amazing she turned out so well."

"Yes. And she still calls Grandma once a week, even though she spends the whole time bitching about Tacoma breaking her heart."

"And that's why you love her."

"One of many reasons."

Shelly smiled and looked out over Commencement Bay, where a tug was drawing into the harbor.

"One reason I wanted to take you somewhere nice, Shawn, is that... I'm afraid I've run out of house. And I did want to thank you for making it look so lovely. Perhaps next summer we can start on the outside. I hope you'll be all right, finding work."

"I'll be fine. But I'll never have as much fun. You're a dream client, Shelly. And don't think I'm going to disappear, just because I'm not working for you."

"Just as long as the neighbors don't talk."

The waiter brought their dishes and Shawn dug in, savoring the lemon and basil on his swordfish.

"Richard's coming back," said Shelly.

"Richard? In-jail Richard?"

"He's being paroled. I've agreed to let him move back in."

"Is that... wise?" asked Shawn.

"No. But... Tacoma loves her grandma, and I love my son. He'll be taking regular drug tests, and staying in the basement, where I can keep an eye on him. And, this may be difficult for you to process, Shawn, but Richard's found religion."

"Call me a cynic."

"We're not all as strong as you, Shawn! Some people need rules, discipline, a promise of heaven or hell. Look at Tacoma's childhood — don't you think she needed it?"

Shawn realized that Shelly was debating with him — seeking his approval for a foolish act. He wasn't about to withhold it.

"Okay. Just as long as you're tough," he said.

"As nails," said Shelly, snapping her lobster tail.

Gold

"I like the mustard skirt better. It hangs better on your hips. How about with the brown knit top?"

Tacoma smiled. "I can't believe I have a boyfriend who actually expresses opinions about clothes."

"You ask, you get."

"Are you sure you're not gay? Don't answer. I'll be right back."

Tacoma headed back to the dressing room. Shawn noticed a rack of tunics, half-price.

"With the rain, I'm not getting much work. And I need to get some new drums for the recording. It's just not a good time."

Tacoma ran down a list of arguments. "I'm dying to ski. The snow is great right now. But if I go without you, I'll be totally bummed." She paused. "What if I pay?"

"You're sure?"

"Yeah! It'll be fun. And I've got money, darn it — I should enjoy it."

"Okay, but..."

"But my ass! You're coming, slave boy. We'll need my car for the skis, but could you drive? I'm no good at mountains."

"Let's try Matador. Here, sweetie. Give this a sniff."

Tacoma's bachelor reform program continued. To Shawn it smelled of branding one's cattle, marking one's territory. But he also understood Tacoma's special talent. She could smell a sprig of lavender at a thousand paces. She liked to sniff him all over and tell him what he'd been doing that day: hiking at the waterfront, hanging out at the Kickstand, rehearsing with the band. If they ever married, he would have to resign himself to never getting away with anything.

"Ooh! Cavalier. That's you all over, Chucho. Nah, too sweet. How about that, with the blue cap?"

The sales ladies of Pierce County's finest retail establishments were being worked hard. This was the fourth department store they'd been to that morning. Tacoma sprayed a whiskey-colored liquid on her wrist. "Ooh! Huh-nee. Try this."

He leaned over and took in a scent with equal measures musk and eucalyptus. It was called Livan. And from then on, this was what he would wear.

"That snow! So icy. It was like a hundred mosquitoes biting my face!"

They went straight for the Mt. Bachelor quad chair, not realizing they were headed straight for the top. They found themselves above the treeline, where the wind was blasting the snow into broad patches of ice. But just as you got your edges into one, you would strike a drift of powder and flop over like one of those inflatable punching clowns. It took them two hours to get back down, and by then the falling snow had turned into sleet.

"This chili is paradise! Do you think we'll get back out there?"

"I think I've had enough," Shawn said.

Tacoma approached an older gentleman at the next table.

"Excuse me. Could you take a picture of us?"

"Certainly," the man said, with a vaguely British accent. "Is this one of those one-button jobs? Ah."

Tacoma plopped down in Shawn's lap and turned to the camera.

Shawn flung out his hand in surprise and broke out laughing. The camera flashed. The man smiled. It was their favorite shot.

"Could I see that one?"

"Certainly."

A gold heart with a king's crown, held between two hands.

"What do you call this?"

"A claddagh," said the salesman. "It originates from a town of the same name, near Galway. You'll find its meaning on that little tag."

Shawn turned over the price tag. *Let love and friendship reign.*

"Good for a girlfriend?" he asked.

"Only if you like her."

"I'll take it."

It was only December 3rd, but Shawn knew a Christmas present when he saw one.

"Honey, could you spot me enough for these cigars? It'll help keep me alert."

"Sure, sweetie."

They left the mountain store and drove a mile before hitting the backup. The snowplows were still working the pass. Shawn took a drag, watching the smoke roil against the windshield.

"You sure you don't mind?"

"It makes you look manly," she said. "Like Ernest Hemingway."

He took another drag and pushed Mazzy Star into the tape deck. Lulled by the slow country blues, Tacoma drifted off to sleep. Watching her, curled against the back of the seat, he felt the ache of a moment that refused to stand still, and he couldn't quite believe how much he loved her.

Evergreen

"Oh! Play that back. See? I'm all blatted out."

"I got it!" said Bobby. "Too much juice. You gotta hold back that tremendous gospel-mama voice till the second verse, when you're risin', and takin' to the sky."

"How's the drums on that?" asked Mitchell. He turned one of 72 dials so they could hear.

"Goddamn perfect," said Jimmy, feigning disgust.

"Consider my ass kissed," said Shawn.

"Are you from this planet?" asked Jimmy. "How come you know the changes before we make them?"

"I come from the galaxy Tam Boo Reen."

"So you want to just re-cut the vocals?" asked Mitchell. "I can back off the guitars from here."

Ivy was fighting not to laugh. Mitchell was so heroin skinny. And that spiky Kevin Bacon hairdo! She wanted to take him in her arms and gently yank him out of the '80s.

"Yeah, that's fine," she said, half-snickering. She took a U-turn down the hall and returned to the voice booth, where a circle of mesh dangled in front of the mic like a noodle strainer. She slapped on the headphones and heard Mitchell's voice.

"Give me a minute to line it up. We'll start from the blues lick."

"Thanks," said Ivy, closing her eyes. *Minimize gospel mama.* The guitarists sat bass-lead-rhythm on the hallway couch.

"Hey," asked Pancho. "Where's Tito Puente?"

"Prob'ly that bagel place across the street," said Jimmy.

Exiting the studio, Pancho spotted Shawn at an outside table, watching his breath puff up toward the evergreen hills. Pancho sat on the table next to him and studied the overcast.

"Silverdale my ass," he said. "Graysville."

"Yeah," said Shawn.

"You are dead-on, dude. So important to have a good drummer on a recording session."

"Thanks," said Shawn.

"You seem tired, though."

"Company Christmas party."

"You have a..."

"Tacoma's company."

"Oh God! The boyfriend-on-a-stick thing. I hate that."

"A database management company, too. Boh-ring..."

"Yuck. Did you at least get a meal?"

"Braised lamb shanks."

"Fan-say!"

"Yeah," said Shawn.

Pancho went inside and bought a croissant. When he returned, Shawn was back to watching his breath.

"So what's the problem?"

"Figured out a good strategy," said Shawn. "Find a guy with an earring. Guy with an earring has to be halfway cool. This guy Mark was dragged along on boyfriend duty, too. And he plays guitar! Funk band. Hung out with him a good half-hour while the girls were makin' the rounds, kissin' corporate butt."

"Pretty funny," said Pancho.

"Turns out Mark's girlfriend and Tacoma are best buds. We head up to their room for some Schnapps. Turns out Mark also has a pierced prick."

"He showed you?"

"Nah. His girlfriend told us. No reason not to believe her. I just..."

Shawn quit the sentence as if he never started it.

"So what's the problem?" asked Pancho.

Shawn emitted three more puffs of breath. The puffs joined up and set out for the sidewalk.

"Tacoma's never had her own money before, and she's got every right to enjoy it. But she calls and says, Honey, let's do this, and let's do that. All these expensive things. So I have to say, 'I can't,' in that dreadful, pathetic tone, and now she's in the position of paying for the both of us or not going at all. It's like this smelly, annoying house guest, always in the room, stirring up trouble."

"That sucks," said Pancho.

"Yeah, and I got my resentments, too. Without Tacoma, I'd still be broke but I'd be having the time of my life. For Christ's sake! I'm cutting a CD with a sexy new drum kit and a kick-ass blues band. Was that not precisely my life's dream?"

"Yeah," said Pancho. "But, without Tacoma, you'd be... without Tacoma."

"Bingo."

Pancho tried to manufacture a comforting thought, but then he spotted Ivy across the street, waving them over.

"I'll buy you a brewski later, kid. Meanwhile, I think we're back on the clock."

"Gotcha," Shawn said, and finished his coffee.

Sandy

It was a typical Tacoma snow, heavy enough to turn green things white, wet enough to melt on asphalt. All in all, a perfect arrangement. Walking past the stadium, Shawn noticed that someone had walked out an enormous MERRY XMAS, PAUL! on the football field.

He felt wistful. Shelly's home was like a girlfriend he hadn't seen in a long time. He had lost the rhythm of painting in his hands. She came to the door with a definite glow.

"Hi Shawn! Come on in. We're just finishing breakfast."

He had forgotten about Richard. He would have been surprised, regardless, because the big bad drug dealer looked more like an accountant: bald but for a horseshoe ring of blond-gray, prominent ears, light-blue eyes, and generous lips that tilted when he smiled. He stood and shook Shawn's hand.

"I was just saying how nice the place looks. You're quite the painter."

"Thanks. It's good to meet you."

Richard ducked his head shyly and returned to his cornflakes. Shelly pulled a black sweater around her shoulders.

"I was thinking we could go to Tully's. I love walking in the snow."

"Isn't Richard…?"

"No, no. Richard's fine. I told him we'd be gossiping, and you can't properly gossip with one of your children around."

Richard waved. Shawn waved back, and followed Shelly into the white world.

Two nights later, Ivy and the Swingin' Richards played Cole's, which had become a twice-monthly gig. They were into the final set, feeling their way through a medley of John Lee Hooker's "Boom Boom" and Pat Travers' "Boom Boom (Out Go the Lights)." Shawn was fighting the tempo, because he was being psychically interfered with. Something in the room was fucking with him, but he couldn't see beyond the stage lights. It wasn't Tacoma — she'd left soon after the first set.

After gigs, Shawn enjoyed having a beer break. It made the loading-up less ponderous, and gave him a chance to let the performance sink in. He went to the end of the bar, where Dina had already set him up.

"Thanks, Dina."

"No prob, shugah. Tell me, though. Why do musicians always drink Samuel Adams?"

"I believe it's a union requirement," said a deep baritone.

Shawn spun around.

"Dad?"

The baritone put out his hands like Al Jolson and said, "Son?"

"What the hell!"

Shawn gave him a boisterous hug, causing him to spill his Manhattan.

"I love you, too, son, but I also had some strong feelings about that drink!"

Shawn unleashed a flurry of play-punches to his father's midsection. His dad doubled over and played the victim.

"Gads! Thou hast delivered me a mortal blow. Art thou a Hercules?"

"This is so cute I think I'll puke," said Dina, then walked off with a whiskey rocks. Shawn's dad eyed her admiringly.

"That one has to be from The Bronx."

"I thought the same thing," said Shawn. "Tacoma born and bred."

"Why, if I wasn't a married man..." He threw Shawn a wink. "You didn't hear that, by the way."

Madison Turk went through life on a small, invisible stage. Given his early career, you couldn't blame him. He worked as a feature reporter for a TV station in Eugene, Oregon, covering the light fare of oversized agriculture products and school principals who sat in dunk tanks for charity. He met Shawn's mom, Helen, at the county fair, where she was named the Lumber Queen.

Feeling a need for stability, Madison conducted a gradual withdrawal from television: first to producing, then to teaching broadcasting at a community college, then out altogether, to direct a Wild West art gallery in Ellensburg.

Madison was also remarkably good-looking. He had chiseled features somewhere between Newman and Redford, thick sandy-brown hair that only recently had begun to gray, and penetrating brown eyes that set all the PTA ladies to half-swoon. It was always odd, knowing that, minus the marriage vows, your dad had a better chance than you of getting laid.

A half-hour later, once Shawn had introduced him to the band ("Your dad's a hottie!" whispered Ivy), Madison finally dropped the shtick and seemed ready to talk.

"So," said Shawn. "How did you find me?"

"Your mother's getting to be quite a wiz on the Internet. She entered your name in a search engine and got a website for blues bands. She was quite proud of herself — and of you."

Shawn studied his beer label, the virile patriot hoisting a stein.

"You guys aren't mad?"

"We miss you, but we're not mad. I did this kind of thing myself – hitchhiked across the country at twenty-three, scared the bejeesus out of my parents. But I had to do it. Hell, I was about to kick you out myself to keep you from turning into one of those Ellensburg boys. I think I figured out the Wendy thing, too."

"Really," Shawn said.

"The old cow-and-milk treatment. Give ya a peek at the udders, then yank 'em away before you get a drop. Maybe a little fire and brimstone, something she learned from the parents."

"Geez. Exactly."

"That's how your mother got me."

"No!"

"Standard practice back then. What she didn't know was, I wanted to buy that cow from the moment I set eyes on her. Please don't tell your mother I referred to her as a cow."

"Sure," Shawn said, laughing softly.

"Funny thing about Wendy. About four months after you..."

"Stop right there, Dad."

"You know where Wendy is?"

"Right here in Tacoma."

"Hot damn! I'm gonna be the hero of the block. I told Rev Fisher I'd ask around."

Shawn smiled. "That's one reunion I'd like to see."

"Speaking of reunions," said Madison. "Your mother wants you home for Christmas."

"Sure, I'll be there. Can I bring a girl?"

"Oh-hoh! What's her name?"

"Tacoma."

"You're dating the city?"

"Um... let's get another drink, Dad."

"Sure. And by the way, could you explain this 'Swingin' Richards' thing? Apparently, it's some sort of double entendre."

White

> The noble Duke of York
> He had ten thousand men
> One day he marched them up the hill
> And marched them down again.

Shawn's sister Beverly sat on the couch, doing the squat-down, stand-up song with her three-month-old, Audrey Nichole. Shawn had never noticed what a pleasant voice his sister had. But then again, he had never heard her sing to her daughter.

> And when you're up, you're up
> And when you're down, you're down
> And when you're only halfway up
> You're neither up nor down.

Tacoma squeezed his hand and whispered, "Adorable."

"Which one?"

"Take your pick."

Shawn sipped from his egg nog, then plucked some needles from the Christmas tree and offered them to Tacoma.

"Smell."

"Mmm. Blue Spruce. Can I rub this all over your body?"

"Please! My parents are somewhere within this zip code."

"Oh, sure. Wouldn't want them to think we're having sex." Her smile quickly fell. "Do you think they like me?"

"They adore you. I'm more worried about me."

"Why?"

"I skipped town! Flew the coop."

"No. I saw that look in your mother's eye. She was overjoyed to see you. And your dad's a pushover. You should read 'The Prodigal Son.'"

"Hah! Any excuse to proselytize."

"Heathen. Pagan. Egg-nog-stic."

"Bible thumper. Jesus freak. Press-byterian."

They were interrupted by Madison Turk, who leaned his head through the kitchen door. "Shawn! Up for some horseshoes?"

"You shit!" Tacoma whispered. "Weren't even gonna tell me."

Madison took a step inside and laughed. "Got more horseshoe pits than septic tanks in Ellensburg."

"Dad, you're gonna be real sorry."

"Why?"

"Because! She's gonna whoop your butt!"

"Well, bring it on!" said Madison, ducking back outside.

Shawn helped Tacoma to her feet. "See? Adoration."

They started in cold sunlight. By the time Madison eked out a four-of-seven victory, a storm front marched over the mountains like the Duke of York and began peppering them with snowflakes. They spent the remainder of Christmas Eve eating oven-warm chocolate chip cookies and watching curtains of snow drifting through the backyard lights. Tacoma kept using the word "perfect" as a sentence.

The next morning, the family managed to put off the gift exchange till ten o'clock. Tacoma was fixated on the view out the window, a foot-deep blanket of white stretching for miles.

"Perfect. It's just like Pittsburgh, only... less crowded and noisy and dirty."

"Be quiet and open your present," Shawn said. He handed her a small box wrapped in green tartan.

"Let love and friendship reign." She cradled the twin claddaghs in her palm. "How..."

"Perfect?"

"Lovely," she said, and reached up to kiss him.

"Watch out," said brother-in-law John. "You keep that up, you'll wind up with one of these." He held up Audrey, a fresh trail of spit-up at the corner of her mouth.

Beverly, Tacoma and Shawn gathered in the rumpus room, decorated with posters of Nirvana and Soundgarden from Shawn's youth. The wood paneling was rung about with rickety aluminum shelves, piled high with board games no one played anymore. Shawn noticed they were using the "Stud" brand playing cards he had given to Tacoma. He hoped she had removed the joker, a smug-looking horse to which he had attached a dialogue balloon full of sexual innuendo.

Tacoma grinned and slammed her cards to the table.

"Hoosier Daddy!"

Beverly looked confused. "Um... are we still playing gin?"

"Hard to explain," said Shawn, laughing. "Hi Mom. Time for dinner?"

Helen Turk stood at the door, sucking on a pencil. She took it out and tapped it on the back of her neck.

"No. Um... Tacoma? There's a phone call for you, dear. You can take it in the master bedroom, if you'd like some privacy."

"Oh, yes. Thank you. Probably my mom, making her Christmas call."

A half-hour later, Shawn was setting out the silverware when he heard Tacoma calling. She met him halfway down the hall, tears in her eyes, and held him a long time before she could speak.

"Grandma's dying," she said.

The stump sat on the property line between the Turks' and the Fishers'. It was broad enough for two, sheltered by a hedge for privacy, and smoothed out by years of makeout sessions. Shawn had often thought he should make it official and lay down some varnish. He sat and watched the lights of a semi curling down the 82 pass.

Wendy came down the driveway, hands in pockets, and kissed him on the cheek.

"Hi pal. Wanna neck?"

"Better not," said Shawn. "Your daddy's a bible-thumper."

"Tell me about it."

"No. Tell me about it."

She joined him on the stump. A pickup rumbled past. Reading the twosome as a tryst, the driver rolled down his window and let out a raucous "Woo-hoo!"

"Shore do miss the white trash of Ellensburg," Wendy drawled. She rubbed a finger along her naked ear. "I took out all the paraphernalia, which seemed to help. Can't hide the blue hair, though. Caught Mom staring at it a few times."

"I'll bet."

"Still. I give the Rev and his wife some credit. I think they realize I'm back on a probationary basis, and they're trying really hard not to make comments. Hope they don't bite their poor tongues off. How's Tacoma?"

Shawn kicked the backs of his feet against the stump.

"Saw her off an hour ago, pumped up on coffee. She's got a flight tomorrow at SeaTac. Thanks for the ride back, by the way."

"Sure. Thursday morning okay?"

"Can you hold out that long?"

"I'll try."

"Cool. I am enjoying hangin' with the folks. Makes me wonder why I left."

"I believe that was me."

"Nah. Dad was right. I was looking for an excuse."

Shawn turned his gaze to the northwest, where I-90 rose into the mountains, foothills glowing white under a low-riding moon. He pictured Tacoma driving up the pass, tired, anxious, looking for stations on the radio. Wendy could see the worry in his face, and felt twin pangs of jealousy and affection.

"Shawn?"

"Yeah," said Shawn, snapping to.

"You really love her, don't you?"

Almost subconsciously, he put a hand over his heart.

"Terribly."

Blonde

Shawn spent New Year's Eve under a log rain shelter in Buckley, playing in a drum circle as people walked across beds of hot coals. It was a paid gig, a hundred bucks for two hours. Considering his lonely-boyfriend state, it wasn't hard for Ivy to talk him into it.

If you figured 200 participants at $195 each, Ivy's new-age friend Jordan was raking it in. Shawn only wished he had skipped the seminar, a four-hour avalanche of phrases like "seeking our true potential" and "freedom to be ourselves," slogans that caused him to instinctually check his wallet.

At one point, Shawn couldn't take any more and shot from his seat. "You dumbfuck! I'm starving to death so I can play drums in a blues band! Do I seem like I'm afraid to do what I want in life? You people are wasting your fucking time here!"

Or at least, he wished he had. But he needed the hundred bucks. So here he was, out in the cold air, smack dab in the lahar path of Mt. Rainier, pounding skins as overpaid professionals sauntered through lava beds. The drummers were mostly competent amateurs, but the dreadlocked black guy on the djembe was definitely a pro. He and Shawn took turns spinning solos over the top of the flow.

Shawn occasionally looked up to check out the walkers. Most of them edged up timidly, let the courage build up then strode across in a burst. A few were more brazen, like the full-figured blonde doing The Twist in the number-two bed, letting out various animal noises.

The blonde was Ivy. She came running back to the drums, her face glowing with adrenaline.

"Omigod! Shawn! That was such a rush. Try it!"

Shawn smiled. "Nuh-uh."

"Why?"

He quoted one of the new age guru's instructions: "'If you find that you don't believe in doing this, we would prefer that you didn't.'"

"You don't?"

"Honey, I got my own rush. I'm gonna beat these congas till my arms fall off."

Ivy checked her watch.

"Would you stop for a midnight kiss?"

"No! Already?"

"Yuh-huh."

Shawn took Ivy by the hands and gave her a friendly smack on the lips.

"Oh, honey," she said. "I'm gonna need something a little more memorable than that. Just pretend that I'm Tacoma."

Shawn yanked Ivy to his chest in a tango-grip, then dipped her until her hair touched the ground and gave her lips a thorough working-over. When he pulled her back up, her eyes were larger than before.

"Whew! Lucky girl! I'm gonna run through the fire again."

Shawn returned to his drums, gave the djembe-player a wink, and caught on to the new salsa track. He waited for the old feeling, the hands drifting off, then peered through a timbered window to find the great white face of Tahoma. He thought he could use it as a satellite dish, to transmit his thoughts all the way to his ladylove in Pittsburgh. *Did you feel that kiss, honey?*

Tacoma was spending New Year's preparing her grandmother for death. The rest of the family was busy fighting over the will — or wills, one of which was apparently executed without any witnesses. Tacoma's

Aunt Lana was riding herd on a trio of lawyers, determined to make sure that things went her way.

Tacoma was just as enraged as everybody else, but realized that someone had to stay out of the fray and see to the old lady's last days on earth. By doing so, she basically relinquished any chance at seeing a dollar, but she was determined to keep her grandmother free of the familial storm, her eyes fixed firmly on heaven.

In his harsher moments, Shawn couldn't see how the old hag deserved such treatment, considering the years of hell she sicced on her granddaughter. But he also understood that his girlfriend possessed a soul of exceptional size, grace and forgiveness.

A month after her grandmother's death, they were sitting on Tacoma's bed, talking about small things, when Shawn was struck by a thought.

"Do you know that... even if we don't end up in each other's lives, even if outside forces should eventually come between us... Do you know that I will always love you?"

To him, it was a simple statement of fact. The sun's out today. Olympia is the capital of Washington State. But on Tacoma, it had a dramatic effect. At first she looked stunned, as if he had just insulted her. Then she seemed to fall in on herself; she turned her back to him and began to sob uncontrollably.

Puzzled, he went to the end of the bed and wrapped his arms around her shoulders. She cried for fifteen minutes, and he knew better than to say a word.

Hunter

Shawn sat on Shelly's roof, taking in a blimp's-eye view of the stadium. He wondered if she'd ever had football parties up here.

I am an autodidact, he thought, trying out a new word. He stretched his legs over the asphalt shingles and considered today's lesson, The Importance of Illusion. Take this trim board, sticking out an inch further than the clapboards underneath. He used to lie on his back and painstakingly paint the underside edge. Later, standing back, he would spot the little squibs that snuck onto the clapboards anyway.

Now, he made his color-break at the natural corner of the board, letting his brush run off the edge into open air. Voila! Straight, sharp lines. And nobody had to know that he'd cheated.

It also occurred to him that he was getting way too analytical about this. But then, he was doing a hell of a lot of painting. The residents of Tacoma had a home-improvement switch that flipped on sometime in March, and word of Shawn's one-man operation was getting out. After Shelly's exterior (blue-gray with white trim), he had a three-tone Victorian in Gig Harbor, then a couple of bedrooms in Spanaway. The first was a friend of Ivy's dad, the second a regular at the Kickstand. How funny that he would be making so much money so soon after breaking up with Tacoma. Or she with him, he couldn't remember.

"Hi!"

"Richard! Geez, you scared me."

"I'm attempting to master my fear of heights," said Richard. He stood with his neck at the gutter line, looking like a decapitated head. "It's not working. How do you do this all day?"

Shawn applied the last touch to an air vent. "I envision all the spine-mangling injuries that might occur if I slipped."

"I... I don't think that would help."

"Ah, but we come from opposite ends of the problem. My weakness is overconfidence, yours anxiety."

"So you practice negative affirmation."

"I am an autodidact," said Shawn.

Richard ignored the verbiage and hefted a large plastic jar onto the shingles.

"What the heck is that?"

"Macadamia nuts. Mom thought you could use a snack."

"Me and what army?"

"Uncle Marty went to Hawaii. I'm allergic to nuts. Well, I better go, before I verti-go."

"Wait," said Shawn. "Can I ask you a question?"

Shawn wasn't even sure what the question was. Richard spent the pause shuffling his feet on the ladder.

"Is... is it working for you?"

"Is what working for me?"

"Christianity. Has it helped?"

Richard looked across the street. The scene of the crime.

"Yeah. But it's not easy. In a perfect world, you'd develop a moral compass long before you're tested. Like building up your strength before a fight. I'm trying to re-learn my lessons, courtesy of the scriptures, but I'm always putting them to use before I'm really ready. I'm literally surrounded by my old life — temptations everywhere. And it's pretty freakin' amazing to look back at it now. Just how far gone do you have to be to sell meth to a teenager a hundred feet from your mother's porch?"

Shawn laughed. "That would take some cojones."

"And there's the biggest temptation of all: concluding that your sin is so egregious that you're beyond salvation. Damn powerful excuse for sinking even lower. Which is why you need to accept forgiveness... even when you don't deserve it, and why you need... why I need, the book and the church and Jesus Christ himself to keep me on track."

"So you might say, you're pulling out the big guns."

Richard smiled. "Exactly. But yaknow? I'm not counting on Him to save me if I fall off this ladder, so I'm gettin' the hell off."

"Hasta la vista, amigo. And thanks for the munchies."

The sun had worked its way through a long train of clouds, and was splashing the roof in sunlight. The splendor of Northwest sunshine was well worth the long drizzles, but this is a secret the locals seem intent on keeping.

Shawn envisioned a moral compass – right, wrong, east and west – and wondered if his was properly aligned. Technically, yes. He was a free man, and had acted with the best of intentions. Emotionally, maybe not. That morning, for the first time since moving to the city, he woke up with a woman who was not Tacoma.

He had taken the day off, because he had a gig that night, and didn't want to wear himself out. A month of brushwork had caused his middle finger to go numb, which could not be a good thing. Faced with an open morning and scads of dirty clothes, he settled on doing his laundry.

He arrived in the basement to find Angie, swatting clothes into a dryer, wearing a T-shirt that did not entirely hide her floral panties. Shawn made a scuttling step so as not to surprise her.

"Finally decided to wake up, huh?"

"Sure," he said.

"Oh!" Angie turned with a start. "Shawn! I didn't know it was you."

"Okay," said Shawn, puzzled.

"Why do you still use your suitcase for laundry, sillyboy?"

"You've seen the size of my apartment. Suitcase or laundry basket – but not both."

"Just be careful. This hallway is the favorite dumping-ground of departing tenants. Andrew is pretty quick to haul stuff away. Four smelly mattresses last week."

"Yeesh!"

Angie slid her quarters into the machine and smiled. "Now get over here and give me a proper greeting."

"My pleasure."

Shawn held their embrace a little longer, enjoying the vanilla scent of Angie's hair.

"Jesus, woman! Can't you wait till I'm gone?"

He was a thin, wispy-looking guy with a Deadhead beard and long, tied-back hair. He wiped away any ill intent with a practiced grin.

Angie burst out in giggles. "Jason! This is Shawn, the guy I told you about."

"Cool," said Jason. "The guardian angel." Shawn shook his hand, noting that Angie's apartment door, previously closed, was now open.

"I told him about the Great Windshield Attack," Angie said, then smiled sheepishly. "Jason's decided to become a permanent fixture."

Jason wrapped a hand around Angie's waist and gave her a possessive kiss. "That's Angie's way of saying we're moving in together."

"Wow!" said Shawn. "Congratulations! What do you do for something like this? Send a card?"

"Maybe we'll have a shack-up shower," said Angie.

"Well hey," said Jason. "Gotta race. Nice meeting you. Bye, hot stuff."

He kissed Angie and left through the basement exit. Shawn waved, feeling awkward.

"Nice guy."

"He's a landscaper," Angie said, investing the word with the cache of *nuclear engineer* or *brain surgeon*. "Oh, but I shouldn't... go on about..."

Shawn was touched by the thought. "Come on, Angie. I had a marvelous romance. Now it's your turn. If anything, it's good to see love and biology still working their magic. Hey! Let's do dinner next week. I'll interrogate the little bugger and give him my blessing, anyway."

"That would be great!"

"Well," Shawn said. "I'd better start my laundry." He pulled his suitcase next to the washer.

"And I'd better put on some decent clothes," said Angie. By way of parting, she settled a hand on Shawn's shoulder. He felt the imprint on his skin, all the way up the elevator.

Two hours later, he stood in the Kickstand bathroom, critiquing the paint job as he peed. *Not bad, but they didn't get all the way behind the toilet tank.* There was a thing for that, called a "long johnny," a skinny roller with a long handle. *Or it could be*, he thought, *I'm getting way too obsessive about this shit.*

Halfway down the hall, he heard someone crying. It came from the back room, a red-painted Chinese number they called the "opium den." Seated on a high-back wicker chair, head in hands, was Wendy. Shawn put a hand on her shoulder.

"Hi," he said. "What's up?"

"Hi Shawn." She looked up with red-rimmed eyes and a sad smile. "Lies. Goddamn lies, biting me in the ass."

"Pancho?"

"No," she said. "Me."

He pulled up a black ottoman and sat down.

"Forgive me," he said. "But what the hell are you talking about?"

"I wish I knew." She laughed and pulled a Kleenex out of her purse. "Gordon's sweet, and wonderful, and charming and handsome, everything I should..."

"Forgive me," said Shawn. "But who the hell is Gordon?"

Wendy let out a snort. "You didn't think his real name was Pancho, did you?"

"Well, I..."

"Oh!" Wendy shrieked. "Don't confuse me. Just listen, okay? I came to Tacoma to get away from my parents, and religion, and all that socially conventional behavior, right? So first thing, I meet a nice boy and fall in love. What the fuck is that? A Frank Capra movie? So Gordon... Pancho, wants us to be exclusive, and I tell him no. Do I have a good reason? No! I've just got my little agenda, and you gotta stick to the agenda. Otherwise you might end up being happy! What am I doing to myself?"

She fell into another crying jag. Shawn squeezed in next to her and pulled her head to his chest.

"Knew this guy," he said. "Left his hometown to get away from this pricktease Christian girl. So he moves to the city, where he falls in love with a Christian girl. Getting my drift?"

"Yeah. You're an idiot, too."

"The King of Idiots. On the other hand, if you force yourself into a relationship with Pancho just because it makes sense, you'll probably take it out on him later. Frankly, he deserves better."

Wendy wiped her eyes. "So what happened with the Christian girl?"

"Don't know," said Shawn. "This weird thing about money, and then he fell in love with music, and she got sucked in by her obnoxious family. Neither of them had any energy left for each other."

For no logical reason, Wendy was now grinning like a maniac.

"What?" he said.

"You heard of the expression 'maintenance screw'? 'Friendly fucking'? 'Booty call'?"

"Well, I..."

"Come on, honey, you owe me one. It's the only thing that's gonna make me feel better. There's a nice comfy couch in the back room, and I give a blowjob like nobody's... Oh God..." She studied his expression. "The neutral gaze of the ethical male. Shit." She grabbed her purse and took flight, stopping at the door without turning.

"I really love you, Shawn, but once in a while, couldn't you just be a penis?"

A half hour later, studying the trails of nutmeg at the bottom of his cappuccino, Shawn found his reasons. First, he couldn't do that to Pancho. Second, there was Tacoma, and the upping of standards. It wasn't that a jump in the sack was no longer in his repertoire. But the first time back, it would have to be for a better reason.

Because they never gave you the chance? said Tacoma.

He looked at the American flag atop City Hall, fluttering in a slow wind.

I had the chance, sweetheart.

Jessica had been divorced for about a year, and she was ready to get back into dating. Shawn came by to give a bid on a paint job, but she seemed more interested in self-analysis.

"I'm a human light switch, on/off. When I got married, fifteen years ago, that side of my personality just disappeared. My ex-husband has an advantage — he didn't give up dating *during* the marriage. Which leaves the sexy but slightly overweight Jessica in her current predicament."

Hello, Mrs. Robinson, Shawn thought. *Note how she fishes for the compliment.* He asked to use the bathroom, found photographs of a younger, slimmer Jessica on the counter. She had been, in fact, a babe. Could you sleep with someone for what they used to be?

Jessica led him upstairs to the master bedroom, hexagonal with a trio of large windows. The walls were covered with a dark, mealy-looking green.

"Everything in the house is so girly-pastel that Jeff insisted on something masculine for the bedroom. We laid down a kelly green, then sponged it over with hunter, and now it looks like a stinkin' jungle. I swear at night you can see snakes. What is so funny?"

"Sorry," he said, still laughing. "Stinkin' jungle. Struck me funny."

"Oh, that. I was starting to swear too much around the kids, so now it's stinkin' this, and stinkin' that."

Shawn had already switched to numbers. *Two coats to cover the color, no trim, popcorn ceiling...*

"How's a hundred and forty? That includes the paint."

Jessica flounced on the bed, showing off an ample but likable ass.

"Money's kinda tight," she said.

Great. Mrs. Robinson without the cash.

"Tell you what," he said. "I always leave a little room in my estimates for unexpected obstacles. Let's call one-forty the absolute ceiling. If everything goes smoothly, I'll drop the price accordingly."

"Deal." She popped up on her knees, displaying an ample bosom.

"Mom! Are we havin' dinner soon?"

The question was followed by a boy with ragged blond hair — seven, eight years old.

"Charley! This is Shawn. He's going to eradicate the rain forest."

"But I like the rain forest! It's dark, so you can sleep better."

"He's got a point," Shawn said.

"Charley, the jungle is giving your mother nightmares. Now go wash your hands. Dinner's in five."

Charley stomped down the stairs, shouting, "Save the rain forest! Save the rain forest!"

"Cute," said Shawn.

"Cute like a Gestapo. But he is the only man I'm currently getting along with. So tell me. How is 'the scene' out there?"

Given recent events, Shawn felt profoundly unqualified to answer. But he gave it a try.

"It's like business. If you want to maintain a strong negotiating position, you have to be willing to walk away from the table. If your primary motivation is the fear of going home alone, you'll end up going home with a long line of freaks.

"On the other hand, if you learn to cultivate your solitude, and treat good companionship as a small miracle, you may just find someone to worship you — which is exactly what each of us deserves. And stay away from drunks, especially the ones who say they hardly ever drink."

"Such wisdom!" said Jessica. "Are you sure you're not fifty? Although I have no idea what could be freakier than a husband who wears his wife's clothing. Oh God. Did I just say that?"

"'Fraid so," said Shawn. "Tuesday all right? Ten a.m.?"

"My. You're unflappable. Tuesday's fine."

On the way out, he met Summer, a skinny, morbid-looking 13-year-old who looked like anything but her name. She responded to his introduction with three unintelligible words.

They stood in the front yard, exchanging the usual pleasantries, when the ex-husband pulled up in his pickup. He was in the neighborhood, dropping by to check on the kids' weekend schedule. Jessica felt obliged to introduce them, and to explain the reason for Shawn's being there. Shawn tried to force back the image of Jeff in a yellow sundress, then waited the mandatory thirty seconds before fleeing for the garden gate.

Yikes! he thought. *This place is a goddamn tarpit.*

The gig was at the triangular coffeehouse on 9th Street. Shawn sat at his drums after sound check, peering down the long room at the magic fishtank. Ivy was sitting there with a stunning blonde — a collection of understated, angular lines to go with Ivy's arcs and semicircles.

It was a little unsettling, playing to a sober, visible audience. They sat in rows of chairs, theater-style, and studied the proceedings like they were watching a chess match.

The first surprise came at the end of the first set, when Ivy introduced a guest singer, Autumn Stolling-something, and the knockout blonde took to the stage.

"And don't be alarmed by the looks on my bandmates' faces," said Ivy. "They had no idea I was going to do this." Ivy turned to the band and half-whispered, "'Summertime,' a little slower," and then slipped from the stage.

Pancho took it lighter, as well. Shawn matched him on the snare, stirring his brushes like featherdusters. Autumn perched placidly on her stool. She had clearly been there before.

She came in more soprano than Ivy, more air than earth, and formed her phrases as if she were blowing small glass animals. More jazz, less blues, little touches of Ella and Sarah Vaughan.

The end of the song brought the added applause of discovery, and another surprise: Autumn wasn't going anywhere. What's more, Ivy was standing in line for a mocha. Shawn was about to signal for a break when Autumn turned around and said, "I don't suppose you guys know 'The Girl From Ipanema'?"

A breeze of aha's wafted through the Swingin' Richards, who had wondered all month why they were learning a song so ill-suited to Ivy's voice.

Just as they started, Autumn said, "Don't be thrown off."

By what? thought Shawn, but he was busy forcing his Yankee fingers into a bossa nova, clave off-beats on the rim of his snare.

Autumn began singing — in Portuguese. Shawn was impressed.

But not Bobby Budoric. Stowing his bass for the break, he muttered, "Sounded a little flat to me."

"No, no," said Shawn. "That's the Brazilian style — a little flat and breathy. Sergio Mendes, Julie London, Antonio Jobim, that kinda thing."

"I knew it," said Autumn, appearing over Bobby's shoulder. "The drummer is always the musicologist. And this one plays like a singer."

Shawn found himself looking at eyes the color of Caribbean lagoons. "Is that good?" he asked.

"God yes! You have a way of shaping the dynamic structure, laying down a path for the singer. So attentive."

"It's easy with you," Shawn said. "You're amazing. How do you know 'Ipanema' in Portuguese? And where'd you learn to round up to the notes like Ella?"

Autumn smiled. "Daddy's superb record collection. And you?"

"Buddy Rich, Gene Krupa, Poncho Sanchez. They keep sneaking in vocalists. Let me try this on you: Keely Smith."

"Oh!"

Shawn smiled. "Correct response."

Autumn put a hand on Shawn's chest. "Hey, I gotta say hi to some friends. Can we continue this later?"

"Certainly."

They were soon into the second set, the fervor escalating every time Jimmy Catarino stomped his distortion box. A few couples even ventured to dance on the patch of hardwood in front of the restrooms.

Ivy took the mic to announce their finale, "Sweet Home Chicago."

"This is a very special night for me," she said. "Because it's my last."

The room went silent. The band turned into a diorama.

"I've been offered a chance to house-sit in Los Angeles, for nine months, and I guess it's time to get on with my acting career. Even though it wasn't on my agenda, this band has been like... a miracle. I want to thank every one of you for... coming along."

She stopped to wipe a hand over her eyes, and then took a deep breath.

"Can we start this goddamn song before I start bawling?"

Shawn clicked off the four-beat, and Pancho jumped in. The rest of them caught up later.

They adjourned to Ivy's house, where they conducted a half-sendoff, half-wake with the help of her new margarita blender. At three a.m., they gathered at the front porch and, one by one, collected enough momentum to take their parting hugs and drift away. Shawn worried about Pancho driving, but concluded that he was more melancholic than alcoholic. Pancho had a fatalistic view of the life-span of bands, and this was feeding right into it.

Ivy walked Pancho to his car as Shawn stood by the gate, studying Ivy's house. An evening rain had coated the grass in crystals of water, sparking in the streetlight, drilling holes into his heart. Since the breakup with Tacoma, the music had filled the desert spaces of his evenings — and Ivy was the gatekeeper.

He didn't need to turn around; he could hear her coming up the sidewalk.

"Why so sudden?" he asked. "Why didn't you tell us sooner?"

Ivy wrapped her hands around his chest and nuzzled his hair.

"I only heard about the house-sitting two days ago. If I didn't go right away they were going to get someone else." She walked around to face him. "You okay to drive, bubbelah? Need some coffee?"

"I can't go."

"You can't..."

"I'm not going." He walked to the porch and turned around, arms out like wings. "The drummer and the singer, Ivy. Nothing like it. Guitarists are mere chaperones, walking alongside. I'm in front of you, laying cobblestones, building bridges. I've never made music like I have with you. Like 'Cold Shot,' when we stop and head for the hook, and I'm dropping tom-toms like smoke signals, sliding you into the pit. Or 'Help Me,' when Pancho cuts off and I pop the snare; and out of the snare comes you, growling like a nasty Venus from the Sea, churning agony and beauty. Sometimes, I swear, it's like the best sex I've ever had!"

Oh, he'd done it now. She was crying. He met her on the walk and traced the backs of his fingers across her cheek. She took his hand and kissed it, then smiled wickedly.

"Shawn? Wanna try for better?"

The last of the high eaves was done, sharp as a new suit. Still, Shawn wasn't ready to leave. The afterglow was scribbling an alphabet of pink cirrus across the sky. Sometimes he wanted to live up here, vault from housetop to housetop, never touch the ground.

He thought of their second go-round, when Ivy and her Amazon curves had worn him silly, when he and his penis were ready to call it a night.

"Oh no," said Ivy. "We're not done with you yet." She slipped off his condom, washed him with a warm cloth, and then set to reviving him with her tongue. What came next, as she rolled on a condom and climbed aboard, was like sending your Johnson through a washing machine. He came in a matter of minutes. Ivy stayed there, gathering her senses, and then rolled to his side, kissing him and smiling.

"A matter of pride," she said.

Shawn plucked a stray bristle from his paintbrush. *Leave it to Ivy*, he thought, *to do the job right.*

He noticed the tablespoon of white at the bottom of his painting cup, found a spot under the front gable, and drew out the letters "SPT" across a shingle, where only he and the occasional seagull would see it.

Red

Three months later, he was back at the fishtank, watching the farmer's market across the street. There was only one farmer, really. The rest were antiques, homey knick-knacks and artwork too bent on customer service to be art. But it was mostly his mood speaking (he had actually bought some lemongrass soap there the week before).

The morning was so bright it was piercing. But Shawn was depressed, and determined to stay that way. It was a miracle he had managed to drag himself out of bed.

They had never realized how important Ivy was, not just as a singer but as a motivating force. Shawn proposed they sign up Autumn, assuming this was what Ivy had in mind with her little "guest vocalist" trick. But the band had no interest in jazz. In fact, it seemed to be headed in the opposite direction — toward the metal blues of Zeppelin, AC/DC and Cream.

They tried out a few vocalists, but afterward would systematically eliminate them with a battery of nit-picks. Their main crime was that they were Not Ivy. They hadn't practiced for a month now. Shawn could feel the rhythm calcifying in his hands.

He thought of offering his services to Autumn. He went up to see her at Jazzbones and found that her piano-bass combo now included a drummer – Claude, skinny black guy with many more chops than Shawn. Afterward, Shawn was paying the usual compliments to Autumn when she introduced her husband. Married at 19? What the hell was the deal with that?

And then there was poor Pancho. Jesus.

Second item: money.

The painting gigs went on for quite a while, but Shawn's car had a nose for cash. He and Pancho went to see Primus at the Tacoma Dome, and were stranded for three hours before the tow truck arrived. Transmission. One thousand big ones. After that, the painting jobs began to dwindle, and he could sense that old scratching feeling. He thought fondly of a month ago, when he could enter a restaurant without first doing the math in his head.

The obvious thing was to get what musicians call a J-O-B, but he hated the idea. He came here to play drums — and had, in fact, done just that. But it was the painting that allowed him to do it. Hard to give up on a dream you've already lived.

Wendy was pregnant. When Shawn went to visit, he could see the film of dust on Pancho's guitar. They hadn't yet decided on marriage, but Pancho being Pancho, he immediately took two jobs, one at a construction site, the other as a dishwasher. It's a natural inclination to want to be joyous at pregnancies, but Shawn had his doubts. He only hoped that Wendy would rise to the occasion, and stop living life only to shock her parents.

God, he couldn't even stay on a subject. Money? Time? Too much time to sit around fretting about money? Shawn eyed his half-gone latte. He should've gotten a coffee.

There was a rapping on the glass. Angie stood at the window, wearing a clownish grin. Shawn managed to raise a hand from the table. Angie skipped through the door and gave him the embrace that had salvaged many a day.

"Hi. How are you?"

"I'm okay," she said, not meaning it. She sat and spread out a pile of small bags. "Little show and tell?"

"Sure."

"Okay. Lovely red sarong, or perhaps large scarf, or small tablecloth, with gorgeous Celtic designs."

"Nice."

"Nifty little wall vase. See? You hang it by this wire, stick the flowers in this little pocket. And then some vanilla-scented lip balm made from hemp. Don't ask, I have no idea. Lastly, some handmade lemongrass soap."

"That's funny," said Shawn. "I..."

"I know. It's for you."

"Really? That's very nice of you."

"When I saw you over here all dopey-looking, I knew I'd better buy you something sweet-smelling before you turned into an Edward Hopper painting."

"Gee," said Shawn. "And here I thought I was doing such a good job of hiding it." He lifted the citrus tang to his nose.

"You're a wallower, aren't you? Wallower! How come so blue?"

There are times when the right question, asked by the right person, can trigger more strategizing than a chess tournament. Angie was back on the market. Turns out Jason was into free love, and was planning to use Angie's apartment as a way-station between conquests. When she found out, he was out faster than an honest politician.

So if Shawn pretended he wasn't stuck on Tacoma, he might have a chance with Angie. But he knew he lacked the energy to maintain the lie.

"Tacoma," he said.

"Oh, Shawn," Angie cooed. "You still miss her, don't you?"

There was nothing women found more attractive than a man who yearns for a lost love. For a guy like Jason, it would be a great way to get laid.

"It's not supposed to last this long," said Shawn. "She's a stubborn virus."

Angie responded with a sigh.

"Oh, stop that!" said Shawn. "You women and your goddamn romance novels."

"Hey, cut me a break. Mine was more like the Jerry Springer show."

"Yeah, sorry. But we've tried this Tacoma/Shawn thing twice now, and I think I need to find a nice atheist girl. And it would be nice to have a band." He dumped his chin on his hand for effect.

Angie caught a glance at the clock. "Oh, God. I gotta get back to work. Can I ask you a favor, though?"

"Shoot."

"I have to go to a wedding in Port Orchard in September. I do *not* want to go by myself. Would you be my date?"

"Yeah, sure," said Shawn. "Maybe spending a day with a hot babe on my arm will do me good."

"Well!" said Angie. "I see your blarney is still intact."

"Blarney nothing. You're beautiful, Ang."

Shawn's sincerity caught her off-guard. She looked like she was about to cry. She gathered up her bags and gave him a kiss on the cheek.

"Thank you," she whispered.

He watched as she looped around the fishtank, then back up St. Helens with a parting smile. The recorded bells of Old City Hall rang out one o'clock. One more hour, done away with.

Royal Blue

Shawn didn't know he had tipped the hammer until it clanged on the concrete twelve feet below. He peered over the railing to find Pancho's eyes, dark and put-upon.

"You're lucky," he said. "Six inches south and you woulda hit the monitor."

They were working at a high-tech firm in Fife, and had been extra careful with the shipping department's new computer, covering it with a cardboard box to fend off the dust. Shawn watched as Pancho mapped out the copper piping, snugging it to the beams with a battery of T-joints, 45s and 90s. He could see why Pancho was already a crew chief.

It took Shawn another five minutes to realize the hammer wasn't his fault. Seeing it on the railing, he had removed it to a table ten feet away. Whereupon Richard used it on some staples and put it right back on the railing.

"Gentlemen!" said Pancho. "We are done. Clean up everything and let's get the hell out of Dodge!"

"Groovy," said Satch. Satch was Pancho's number two, and he worked all day wearing a cell phone with a headset. "Three o'clock's a fine quittin' time, dontcha think, Dickie?"

"Sure," said Richard, smiling shyly.

They were getting into Shawn's car when Richard said, "Thanks, Shawn."

"Aha! I'm glad you noticed, you scumbum."

"Yeah, I'm learning things. Heavy hammers, thin railings..."

"'Salright. Pancho's a bandmate. He won't hold it against me.

'Course, if it had hit that monitor, I'da ratted on you in a second."

Richard laughed. "Duly noted."

They took the frontage road and headed downtown.

"By the way," said Richard. "My mom's got some German chocolate cake. And she's not taking no for an answer."

"I wouldn't ask her to." He turned onto 705, drinking in the skyscrapers.

Shelly seemed flustered. After doling out thick slabs of cake with milk, she excused herself to make a call. When she came back, Shawn and Richard took turns exaggerating the flying hammer story.

"Well, Pancho's got this incredible peripheral vision – used to play soccer when he was younger – and right before the hammer skulls ole' Satch, he reaches out and..." The doorbell rang. "Oh, um... You want me to get that, Mom?"

"No, I've got it, dear."

It was Tacoma. Her astonished smile revealed the breadth of Shelly's deceit. Shawn found himself rising to his feet.

"Richard," said Shelly. "Give your mother some working space."

Before leaving, Richard whispered in his mother's ear: "I expect a full report."

Shelly turned to Tacoma and said, "Cake, dear?"

Tacoma broke her eyelock with Shawn. "Yes. That would be great."

Shelly left the room. Shawn and Tacoma sat down at the table.

"Hi," said Tacoma.

"Hi," said Shawn. "How's it going?"

"Okay. I quit my job."

"Really?"

Shelly burst through the door. "Here you are, dear. And don't be like those other girls who pretend they don't like food."

"No problem there, Shel."

Shawn noted the shortening of the name, and raised an eyebrow in Shelly's direction.

"Okay, Shawn. I suppose you deserve an explanation. After all this time you and Tacoma have been getting together and breaking up, I decided I had to meet her. She wasn't hard to find — there aren't too many Tacoma Davenports in the phone book." She began to snicker. "Sorry dear. In my youth, you would have been a sofa shop."

The stunned boy and the nervous girl were much too preoccupied to get the joke.

"Well. Yes," said Shelly. "City Girl and I began having lunches once, twice a week, and she gave me the same story I've been getting from you. The tremendous void in your life, the feeling that your relationship was under constant attack from outside forces: bipolar episodes, financial setbacks, deaths in the family."

Shelly stood and paced like an attorney.

"Well, you two — I'm sick of the whining! This is what life does to people who fall in love. You have to learn to fight it out."

She was getting too excited, so she sat down and sipped her coffee.

"Because he is dead, and because we never divorced, you probably assume that Francis and I had a perfect, sunshiny marriage. But you weren't there the day he got back from Cleveland and I found a note from 'Rosie' in his jacket pocket. I also found a used pair of panties wrapped in a sandwich bag. I don't know which I hated worse: the betrayal, or the stupidity of not hiding the evidence."

"It took years for him to regain my trust, and lots of messy, noisy fights. Not because we wanted to fight, but because that was the only way we could save our marriage. Fighting requires passion; passion means you care."

She patted two fingers against her temple, trying to recall her next point.

"The other thing is this: Shawn," she put a hand on Shawn's elbow. "I love you almost as much as my own son. In a very difficult time, you brought life into my house, and gave me someone to talk to. Now you've even gotten my son a job. You're a wonderful, sweet young man, and you deserve the best. 'The best' is precisely that woman sitting across the table from you. A person doesn't go through as much living as I have without getting a pretty good idea about people who belong together, and people who don't. Which is why I'm committing this atrocious act of meddling. You two need to give this thing another shot — but you need to stop being so goddamned civilized. Argue, shout, bicker. Break a few ceramics. She's from Pittsburgh, she can handle it. And now... I've got a present."

She went to the front closet and retrieved a box wrapped in purple tissue.

"Here, honey. Untie the ribbon, and we'll let City Girl finish the job."

They opened the box to find a royal blue dragon kite with a large spool of string. Tacoma looked at Shelly, quizzically.

"Go fly a kite! At Point Defiance. This afternoon. It'll give you something to talk about. I predict, by the time you get to the end of the string and back, you will have made some progress."

They stood in the green bowl of the park's front lawn, wind whipping off the narrows. The kite found the end of the tether in ten minutes. The effort provided a prelude of small cooperations, making it easier to start.

"So you quit your job."

"Yes!" said Tacoma. The kite veered left, and she gave the line a tug. "I realized... I was doing something I saw no value in. Now I'm tutoring at a literacy center."

"I'm impressed!"

"Thanks. So what're you up to?"

"The band's pretty much dead. I'm working with Pancho, for a contractor. Just gofer stuff, but I hope to pick up some skills. You've heard about Pancho's new wife?"

"Yes! And I hear he's going to be a father, as well."

"He never could do things in the right order."

"Hmmph," said Tacoma. "At least that's one less woman in Shawn's harem."

"Hey! They're all friends and you know it."

"Except Angie. You're attracted to Angie."

"I was. But there is absolutely no chemistry. I told you that."

"I think you're a rake."

"For a rake, I get very little actual sex."

Tacoma handed him the spool.

"Any since me?"

"One. Ivy."

"Ivy! She wasn't even on my list."

"Mine, either. One of those friendly... farewell things. What about you?"

"I dated this one guy. He wanted to kiss me goodnight. I told him I couldn't, because it would remind me of my ex-boyfriend. He seemed... puzzled by that."

"I don't blame him."

Tacoma cast a smile to the grass. "So. Do you like this?"

"This what?"

"Fighting."

"We're not fighting."

"Openly disagreeing. Casting ugly truth to the wind. Like you having sex with your lead singer."

"At the time, I didn't have a girlfriend," he said, a little too sharply.

The comment sank into Tacoma's face, but she let it go. "Now there — that's fighting." She extended a hand for the spool. "We need a name for the kite."

"Hal," said Shawn, thinking of science fiction.

"Nuh-uh. You know what he looks like, don't you?"

Shawn squinted skyward — the circular head, the long, wiggling tail.

"Sperm"

"Spermie!"

"Okay," he said, laughing. "You want to reel in 'Spermie' and go for some espresso?"

"You got it. Friend-fucker."

"Oh! You are mean."

They drove a few blocks to the Antique Sandwich Shop and walked in on the weekly open mic. A young female sat at the piano, reeling out breathy melismas in the current confessional style.

"Some," said Shawn, "should sing with less emotion."

"A-greed," said Tacoma. "You can feel the torment in the air. Was I too much of a noodge?"

"Noodge?"

"Did I pick on you about little things. Did I nag you."

"At times. But I can handle it."

"That doesn't change the fact that I was being a noodge."

"No. Ugly truth."

"In my wacky family, the only way we express love is by nagging. 'Why do you dress so funny, Tacoma?' 'What's the deal with that hair?' 'Why are you studying Russian?' That's why, when we first got together, I didn't believe that you loved me."

"In my wacky family," said Shawn, "we express love by *not* nagging each other."

"Freak!"

"Goddamn Beaver Cleaver, that's me."

"As long as we're confessing," she continued. "That's also why I cried so much when you said you would always love me. No one ever told me that before. I also thought you were saying it... because you were anticipating us breaking up."

Shawn took a long sip from his latte, which was threatening to go cold from all the talking. "In a way, I guess I was. But I do still love you."

Tacoma smiled, little fissures forming all over her heart. She took Shawn's hand and pulled it to her lips. A blond man with a blond guitar sat at the mic, explaining the title of his song.

"It's called 'Grace,' but it's not about a specific person. 'Grace' is the name I use for all the people who come to hear me sing."

"Nice," said Shawn.

"If I ever had a daughter," said Tacoma, "I would name her Grace."

Amber

The inspector said he'd be there by noon. It was three. Pancho stood by the circuit board, whapping a screwdriver handle against his palm.

"Shit! I can't have you guys just sittin' around. Satch? Arnold? Go on home. Me and Shawn'll rewire back to the old circuits. I'll call you later and let you know about tomorrow."

A lot of people might have left the house dark and blamed it on the inspector. Not Pancho. He wanted his clients – the Mendozas – to lead as normal a life as possible. After he was done, he handed Shawn what looked like a chunk of obsidian, pitch black and shiny.

"That's from the old mast. Aluminum wiring. Got so hot it melted the electrical tape into that. No reason at all to use that shit. Cheap bastards. Wanna hit the Queen?"

They followed a maze of industrial streets to the Emerald Queen, an old-fashioned paddleboat steamer parked in the shallows off the Port of Tacoma. Shawn looked forward to seeing which arthritic band was playing there next.

"K.C. and the Sunshine Band. Whoo-ee!"

"Yeah," said Pancho. And check the undercard."

"Steppenwolf?! There is no God."

Shawn veered right at the entrance and dumped five bucks on his favorite nickel slot. If you lined up three fishing lures, you got to pick from five anglers on a video screen. Shawn picked the blond farmboy, who reeled up a tin can worth five nickels. He didn't last long after that, and found Pancho at the three-penny slots, dispensing with his last two bucks the slow way. He looked like he was about to fall asleep.

"How you doin'?"

"Tiny victories, tiny losses," sighed Pancho. "Much like life."

"Thank you, oh sensei. Hey... I been meanin' to ask..."

"Why you don't have more to do?"

"Exactly. Yesterday, I finished the entire New York Times crossword. I feel like I'm stealing money."

Pancho pulled a button and lined up three angels, for 27 cents. "Contractor crews are like SWAT teams. You don't often need every man, but when you do, it's critical. I like to have one guy I can pay a ridiculously low sum – say, a starving musician – to be that extra pair of hands. Don't worry, you'll soon have days when you're working too much. Plus, we're charging man-hours; my boss makes twelve dollars every time you make eight. So relax."

"Okay," Shawn said. "But it might take a while. God, I never thought I'd miss housepainting."

"By the way, if you do get a housepainting gig, take it. I'm flexible. Besides, when he's not meeting with his parole officer, I've got Richard, too."

"How'd you get so smart, Pancho?"

"Used to hang with my dad's crew when I was a kid. They'd send me into the crawl space to hunt for wires. Said I was a good mouser."

"Speaking of crawling, how's married life?"

"Very funny, bachelor boy." His machine rang out another jackpot. "See? The angels are with me. Things are going pretty well. Wild hormonal swings. I've learned to take an hour or two away when I can. Oh, and you'll enjoy this: Wendy wants us to start going to church."

"Ha!" said Shawn. "The Christian girls always go back."

"Hey, I don't think it's a bad idea. Let's face it: Wendy's got issues. Church might provide her with a little stability before she goes raising the next generation. What's your trip about religion, anyway?"

"Evangelism."

"Meaning?"

"Some Christians market their beliefs like they're selling fucking Amway. The other night, there's this guy handing out leaflets on Sixth Street. I figure it's flyers for a nightclub, so I take one, and there's a picture of Jesus, and the guy asks me if I go to church. I say no. He asks me if I'd like to talk about it. I say no. He plows on ahead into his Good News spiel, the road to salvation, yada yada. This infuriates me. The guy has so little respect for other people that he's willing to stop strangers on the street and question their beliefs. Isn't that... violent?"

"I wouldn't call it violent."

"How about dreaming up a place where you send everybody who disagrees with you to burn in eternal fire? Is that violent?"

"You got me there. So what did you do with the leaflet guy?"

"I crumpled up his flyer and threw it into the intersection. As I walked away he yelled out, 'God loves you!' I yelled back, 'Well I'm not too crazy about him!'"

"I'm sorry I missed all this."

"Very entertaining."

"So what about Tacoma?"

"She seems... to accept my beliefs for what they are. One time, she told me I was more 'Christian' than most Christians. The way I treat people, that kinda thing."

"I'd have to agree."

"On the other hand, look at Wendy. You can't trust 'em. Sooner or later, they're going to start praying for your soul. I guess that's why I don't feel fully invested right now. We've tried the thing twice and it doesn't seem to work. I'd like us to have three easy months. Then I'll jump in."

"Sounds reasonable," said Pancho. "Here, let me kill this off." He punched up his last 25 cents, got ten devils and one good-for-nothing angel.

It was their weeknight Wednesday. He lay in Tacoma's bed, waiting for her to drift off before he left. He was thinking about Angie. How he had promised to take her to that wedding and that's exactly what he was going to do. And he wasn't going to tell Tacoma, because he didn't want the drama. Three easy months. But fibbing to Tacoma was, to borrow the old expression, like trying to sneak the sun past a rooster.

"Gears clicking?"

Her eyelids rose, amber sparks of iris.

"Hmm?"

"Can't sleep," she said. "Gears clicking. Big factory full of gears. Wassamatta?"

A lot of answers for that. He picked one from the bunch.

"I was thinking how... when I first found out you were bipolar, I thought I was going to be the strong one, and just handle it. I think I underestimated the effect it would have on me. Here's this woman I'm crazy in love with. One night she shows up, and she's somebody else. That's... disconcerting."

"Poor honey," she mewed, and kissed him on the neck. "Did I tell you about the guy at the literacy clinic?"

"No."

"He was a teacher there, nice enough guy. He asked me out, and we exchanged numbers. But I thought I should let him know about the bipolar. When I told him, he asked for his number back."

"God! What an asshole."

"'Salright. Some guys aren't up for it. I'm glad I found out early."

"No," said Shawn. "No one should treat you like that."

"Time for Bubba to leave?"

"Yeah." He kissed her and went off to get dressed.

"Thanks for the kite," Shawn said, sipping Shelly's coffee.

"Not my idea, originally." Her eyes rose. "After the Rosie Affair, I couldn't let go of the betrayal. So I went to a counselor, and she said, You know what you're doing? You're sandbagging. Whenever you and your husband get into a conflict, you pull up all these things from the past and throw them between you until you've built a nice big wall. He's tied up by guilt, you're tied up by resentment, and where have you gotten yourself? So, she said, whenever things get tense in the household, I want you and your husband to go to the park and fly a kite. And I want you to imagine that the kite is your marriage. It only flies by the consent of you, your husband, and the weather. And should you decide to tie a sandbag to its tail, it will plummet to the ground.

"We spent an awful lot of afternoons flying that kite. Of course, we didn't call ours 'Spermie.'"

Shawn held up his hands. "Not my idea."

"I know, dear. It's cute, though. Your own little fertility rite."

Richard came up the stairs, hair still wet from the shower, and they headed out to Shawn's car. He squinted at the bright sky.

"Were you guys talking about fertility rites?"

"Kites," said Shawn. "We were talking about kites."

"Oh. Did the inspector show up yesterday?"

Green-and-White

It was a marvel of multiculture. The bride was half-German, half-Mexican. The groom was Jewish. The ceremony was a fusion of rituals, some Catholic, some Jewish, some entirely original. At the end, their friends tied a dozen scarves together to form a circle around the couple.

They stood on the front lawn of a bed-and-breakfast overlooking the inlet between Port Orchard and Bremerton. The sun had faked out the weathermen all day, eluding clouds like a running back slipping tackles. As the rabbi said the words "husband and wife," two green-and-white state ferries crossed in the water behind them.

For the bridal dance, the maid of honor sang "Fly Me to the Moon," and then gave way to the Kosher Red Hots, a keyboard-clarinet-vocal trio who spun out Jewish folk music and American swing. The singer could scat just like Ella (*although it would be nice*, thought Shawn, *if she had an off-switch*).

A teacher led them through some folk dances, then they dove into a tri-fold buffet: Mexican (enchiladas, taco salad), Mediterranean (dolmas, pitas with hummus) and Northwestern (smoked salmon, Bavarian potato salad). Afterward, Shawn dragged his full stomach back to the lawn, where he joined the mob of young men lofting the bride and groom upon chairs.

This and three glasses of champagne had Shawn pretty worn out, so he and Angie spent the rest of the reception on the gazebo, blowing bubbles at the remaining dancers.

"Call me sappy," said Angie. "But that was the most perfect wedding I've ever seen."

Shawn blew into his wand and sent a squadron of bubbles after the bride's parents.

"I'll bet it's because they're older," Angie continued. "They've had more of a chance to cultivate a personal style — and they don't have to give in to their parents' ideas."

"You know what I hate?" Shawn said. "Those weddings where all the guys wear the same tuxedo, like they're all on a fuckin' football team."

"Let's talk about the three absolutely useless bridesmaid dresses in my closet."

"The idea being to make everybody but the bride look hideous," said Shawn. He passed the bubble-gear to Angie. "If I had a wedding, it would be kinda like this one."

"Uh-oh," said Angie. "Do I hear questions popping in the air?"

"And why is it *popping* the question? You can ask a question, pose a question, raise a question. But when you *pop* a question, it's always the same question."

"Who are you — Jerry Seinfeld?"

"I guess the Jewish wedding is rubbing off."

"By the way, I hope Tacoma didn't mind that you were escorting me. I really do appreciate it."

"She was fine," said Shawn. "She knows you and I are friends. Why do you think we never did... jump in, Angie? I've always thought you were attractive."

"And I, you. But you were always in love with Tacoma."

"Wow. That obvious?"

"Yep."

Shawn swallowed the last of his champagne and gazed over the rooftop, where gray clouds gathered behind the chimney. *It always comes back to Tacoma.*

He felt a drop of rain on his forehead. Angie giggled. He turned to find her holding an empty wand.

"Sorry," she said. "I think I spat on you."

Brown

"Have you had enough?" asked Tacoma.

"Are you allowed to leave?"

"I've done my duty."

They slow-danced in a far corner of the Tacoma Dome, having survived four hours of country music. The tickets came from Tacoma's boss. But Shawn's sense of rhythm had been assaulted long enough.

They walked a few blocks to the Harmon Microbrewery, where the cool, dark interior offered a nice escape from the humidity. Shawn sipped at a wheat beer and noticed a billboard-size portrait of Woody Guthrie at the History Museum across the street.

"Now there's..."

"Yeah."

"I'm sorry. It's these goddamn ears of mine. It's so hard to be non-critical of someone in your own field. But I still can't believe your boss didn't know who Asleep at the Wheel was."

Tacoma smiled. "And this from a woman whose hair is so authentically big, whose truck is so genuinely huge..."

"And who hired three teamsters to get her into those jeans."

"Isn't denim an amazing material?"

"Well," said Shawn, laughing. "I'll give you the Dixie Chicks, but the rest of those fakers are playing pop music with a twang. And that one Generic Love Anthem they keep dragging out... Give me Buck Owens any day."

"Thanks for suffering with me, sweetie. So how was yesterday's excursion?"

"Oh! Let me tell ya. Pancho had a great time. They had this incredible guitarist, young black guy. Pancho brought a pair of binoculars so he could see how he fingered his chords. It was good for him to get away, too. This responsible adult thing has been pretty tough."

"Poor Pancho. How was the drummer?"

"You know, Gatemouth is so straight-ahead, it was hard to tell. He did this one thing with the snare, though, little drumrolls inside the beat. I'm definitely gonna steal that."

Shawn had done his research. But he could tell Tacoma only so many lies before he exploded. He stared at Woody Guthrie's rough-cut face.

"Honey?"

"Oh, uh... yeah. Sorry. Tired, I guess."

"I've got something to take care of that," she said. "Let's go to my place."

She was clearly intent on being nice to him. He was going to have to live with it.

Lately, their sex was not as exciting. Nothing terrible, just the leveling effects of Tacoma's medicine, which took out the peaks as well as the valleys.

That night, she was different — electric to the touch, almost frantic. Every button he pushed brought a small detonation. The outfit didn't hurt, either: a lacy red-and-black number you might see in a western movie.

This was the comfy cellar of pleasure that brought Shawn to his reckoning. He lay at her side, tracing a finger along her shoulder blade, and could no longer bear the distance of small deceptions.

"Honey, this is going to seem silly and stupid, but I didn't go to Gatemouth Brown yesterday. A couple months ago, I promised Angie I would take her to a wedding. But I didn't want to tell you. I just wanted to keep my promise and be done with it."

"So you lied your way around it," she said, without turning.

"Yes. And I'm very sorry, I can see that I was being selfish. And foolish – because you always know when I'm lying."

She twisted around to face him. Her expression was hard to read.

"I'm glad you told me before I had to drag it out of you."

"I know. I just..."

She put a finger to his lips. "Stop. Don't ruin this. We'll talk later."

She turned back around. A minute later, he ventured a hand to tug at her hair – her favorite gesture. She gave herself to the sensation and they made love, this time in silence. Then fell asleep, drifting to their separate sides.

All the next day – Labor Day – he waited for the hammer to fall. He woke up early and made breakfast, a linguisa omelet followed by bowls of sliced mango.

They stopped at the Antique Sandwich Shop for breve lattes, then headed south to the Nisqually Delta, where they walked a long bird trail. Shawn was determined to spot a bald eagle, but had to settle for a pair of great blue herons, sighted through Tacoma's binoculars in the mudflats.

She spent the rest of the walk spinning out questions like a talk-show host. Some of them seemed cold and impersonal, but he was used to it.

"Do you see yourself as someone who needs to be the center of attention?"

"No. But I don't avoid it. Anyone who wants to jump on a stage has to hope at least a bit of an ego."

"So is the ego-trip the main benefit?"

"No. When I make the physical motions of playing the drums, the creation is only halfway there. It's only complete when someone responds to it. Even better, dances to it. You wouldn't believe the power, all those butts and feet at the end of your sticks."

They went on like that, a new question every few minutes. Did he think his drumming would ever fit into a normal lifestyle? Had he ever possessed an image of his perfect mate, and what were her characteristics? (And no BS'ing the interviewer.) Was he spoiled as a child? Neglected? What was the basis of his agnosticism?

"Lack of faith."

"Really?"

"Yes. Kind of a negative phrase, I know? But faith is a thing you either have or don't have. There's no faking it, and you have no choice in the matter. So my agnosticism is not, per se, a rejection of any particular religion.

"Viewed another way, I have much more faith than a religious person, because I am willing to live without guarantees, and to let the mysteries of the universe remain mysterious."

"Well," said Tacoma. "I hope you're right, honey. On the other hand, I guess I don't. Are those swallows?"

By the time they got home, they were both exhausted. Shawn gathered his clothing from the day before, carried it outside in a sack and turned for a kiss.

"I'm sorry. I can't kiss you right now."

"Why?"

"You lied to me, Shawn. No matter the particulars, you lied to me. I'd appreciate it if we didn't talk till... well, just let me call you when I'm ready. I have to think about this."

He tried to think of something he could say to heal this, but he couldn't.

"Good... Goodbye, Tacoma. I... Okay."

He counted each tread on the staircase, raindrops peppering his path. Then he looked back for her face, but could see only the palm of her hand, flat against the screen.

Slate

She called at six o'clock the next morning and made a number of curious observations, the principal of which was, "I feel like you've been neglecting me."

"Honey, I just spent the last two days with you. I went to that godawful concert just to be with you. How could you think I was neglecting you?"

"Sometimes... when we were walking, I'd ask you a question and you wouldn't respond."

"Do you realize how many questions you asked me? You were like Barbara Walters on speed."

"Oh. But sometimes it seemed like you weren't giving me your full attention."

"This happens, you know. Boyfriends don't always hear what their girlfriends say. But I was trying."

"I've got to get to work. I'll call later. 'Bye."

He didn't hear from her for days, and spent his week conducting an unofficial survey of his friends.

Shelly

"No, it was not a smart move, lying to her. But I think it'll work out. Just give her some time. I'm sure she'll realize that it was a foolish lie, not a malicious one."

Pancho

"Dude, she really needs to cut you some slack. You know and I know, the two of you broke up because *you* were poor. But consider the reason you were poor. You were pursuing your life's dream. So, what? She snaps her fingers and you're supposed to be back on her leash? It would be different if you were screwing Angie, but at most you were just testing your feelings. If she's going to hold this against you forever, then the hell with her!"

Angie

"Geez! I guess I'm flattered that she considers me such a rival. Does she realize that you and I always end up talking about her? If you were trying to get me in the sack, that's a pretty piss-poor approach!"

Wendy

"Sorry, man — you blew it. You took a tiny little thing and made it big. That's what's bugging her, yaknow. If this date with Angie was nothin' special, why didn't you just tell her? Then you had to tell all those other lies to cover up Lie Number One. You have to ask yourself, what was so all-fire important about hanging on to this little shred of independence? Weren't you saying, 'No, you can't have all of me yet'? The hell with the blame. Blame gets you nowhere. What are your *actions* telling you about your *feelings*?"

As the biggest screwup on the panel, Wendy naturally made the best point: how *did* he feel about Tacoma? Come Saturday, after five days and no calls, he came to something of a conclusion. He was sitting in a seafood place at Point Defiance, sharing fried clams and a beer with Pancho.

"She kept telling me that a relationship is hard work. But not all the time! Every couple needs to build their story, their mythology, and every mythology needs a paradise, a perfect time. What was our paradise? A month after we meet, she's diagnosed with bipolar!

"So this time, I ask for three easy months. And I'm holding back ten percent of myself as insurance — that's the ten percent that wanted to lie about Angie. And now... she's obviously given up on me, because she hasn't called, and she asked me not to call her. So I'm thinkin', we've done it again, man. The slate is clean."

Pancho had run out of opinions. They sat and watched the ferry pull in from Vashon Island. Shawn's fingers tapped the table in a metronome tic. *Drummers*, thought Pancho. *Even their tension has rhythm.*

"I'll get us another pitcher," he said.

"Okay."

As Pancho walked toward the bar he hit the speed-dial on his cell phone.

"Hello?"

"Hi. Me. All right if I hang with Shawn a bit? He's having a hard time."

"Yeah, sure. Take it easy, though. Your daughter doesn't need a DUI daddy."

"We'll take a kayak. Oh, 'scuse me, hon. Got a call comin' in."

Shawn turned to find Pancho holding a full pitcher and a cell phone. He gave the phone to Shawn.

"Oh... for me? I... Hello?"

"Hi. I'm sorry I haven't called. I'm in the hospital."

Emerald

What went on inside the walls of a house had always been a mystery to Shawn. But it took him by surprise when Pancho told him to drill holes through some studs and tie three outlets to a single wire.

"Wait a minute! How many freakin' things can you tie to a single wire?"

"One circuit, up to ten appliances. After that, you start getting 'nuisance trips.'"

It seemed like something that should have been obvious — but in 24 years, Shawn had never wrapped his mind around this particular thought. Electricity suddenly seemed like an endless stream of power, with a mind-boggling capacity for interconnectivity.

His next assignment was to daisy-chain four can lights in what would eventually be the "piano room." Like everything else that went inside the walls and ceilings, the lights had knife-sharp metallic edges. Especially dangerous, given Pancho's fetish for stuffing as many wires as possible through each drilled hole. Shawn was struggling to pull a third wire through a 7/8" opening. He had six inches through, but the two previous wires were binding together, keeping it from going any further.

Despite yesterday's lessons – two finger-slices and one knuckle-gouge – Shawn was about to initiate a fatal combination. He wrapped the wire around his fingers for added leverage. He also changed the angle of attack, unwittingly freeing the wire from its previous bind. One mighty tug toward the can light six inches away and...

"Shit! Motherfucking son of a... FUCK!"

Pancho leaned in between the studs. "Something the matter?"

"This is the matter!" He showed the C-shaped cut across the back of his hand. "How much fucking blood do I have to donate to this fucking house before I stop doing fucking stupid SHIT like this?! You got a bandage?"

"I'll check," said Pancho. He reappeared with an old sock and a roll of duct tape.

"That's it?"

"Blue-collar Band-Aid," said Pancho. "Here."

Shawn held the tape and stared at his wound, feeling pathetic. "God, Panch. I just feel so stupid when I do that."

"'Salright, man. It's not you — it's your hands. They haven't figured out how to do this yet. Believe me, I've donated a few pints myself. Here, wash it out with this bottle of water, then tape it up, but take a break, too. I don't want you doing this stuff all frustrated and pissed-off."

"Thanks, Pancho." Shawn crossed the back lot to a low stone wall, where he ripped off a strip of cloth, placed it over the cut, then wound the cloth and the duct tape around his hand.

The house stood on a hill in Puyallup, overlooking the downtown, which was just then playing host to the Washington State Fair. Shawn watched the crowds oozing around the fairgrounds, the cars lined up in the parking lots. In the foreground was an evil-looking contraption that whirled people around on either end of a hundred-foot pole. You could hear the screams all day long.

Interconnectivity, he thought. *Why are people drawn to crowds of other people? And who the hell pays somebody to toss them around on a bucket 200 feet in the air? Is life such a dull, numb ache that you gotta volunteer for* this *shit?*

He looked further on to the stripe of the Puyallup River, which was blue, brown or green, depending on your mood and where you caught it. It was the Puyallup Tribe that ran the Emerald Queen Casino and named the mountain. He'd read it on a plaque in Old Town Tacoma. They named the mountain Tacopid, which means, "She who brings us the waters." The waters came down in a river named after the tribe, through a town named after the tribe, past a casino run by the tribe. He realized that the pain in his hand had become a dull, numb ache.

Tacoma called him the day she got home from the hospital.

"I'm going back to Pittsburgh. I need to be with my family, in familiar surroundings. I want to reconnect with my mom, and... I can't help but associate Washington with my sickness."

"Does that include me?" he asked. "This thing with Angie — was that part of it?"

"Love is stressful even when it's good," she said. "So, yes, partly you — but I'd been working too much, and that week I wasn't eating enough. They all come together, and that's how you get an episode."

He said nothing.

"I hate to ask you this, honey, but... could you help me move?"

He spent the rest of the week in constant replays. He'd missed all the signs: the manic interview on the bird trail, the strange call the next morning (the onset of the delusional state). Even the sex – she was much more responsive than she should have been, if the meds were working. And then the trigger – his lie about Angie.

Still, he kept coming back to that odd phrase: *lack of faith*. She had apparently set him up as the state's last chance to keep her, though not fully investing herself in him or it. Then one transgression — Bam! Off to Pennsylvania.

But he didn't have the luxury of blaming her. He could no longer subject her to the poison of an unstable life — his life, the life he wanted. If he changed his life to keep her, he would resent her, and that, too, would poison her.

So, a lack of faith, yes. *But faith is a thing you either have or don't have.*

The following Saturday, he borrowed a company truck and moved her furniture to a storage space. When that was done, they carried a dozen boxes to her car. Someone had smashed a jug of wine in the entryway, leaving a pungent, skid-row smell. He would remember that, but very little of what was said — they were both hesitant to say anything meaningful.

Under a cloudy twilight, he settled the last box into its spot and closed the hatchback. They glanced around nervously.

"Thank you, Shawn. I know it's hard, but I didn't know who else to call."

"It's okay. I'm good for... You're welcome."

She looked flustered for a second, then hugged him and kissed him on the cheek.

"I do love you, Shawn."

"I love you, too."

"Goodbye."

She turned for the entryway, walking quickly. He watched her, thinking, *I have to remember this.* She rounded the corner, a lock of hair, an elbow, a slice of shadow. He would spend the rest of his life missing her.

Also by Michael J. Vaughn...

Tommy Folgett's life is littered with disappointments: a broken marriage, alcoholism, and squandered artistic talent. But he did create one hell of a softball team. Under Tommy's tutelage, this hodge-podge of characters has lived out ten years of victories and defeats, joys and squabbles, on Friday nights at the Double River softball complex. They have, in fact, become a family.

When a broken relationship sends Tommy back to the bottle, the self-abuse spills over to his housemate and shortstop, Honus. Tommy's envy of Honus' writing career, and the campaign of subtle sabotage that follows, threatens to destroy his one great achievement: the legendary Barons.

...available everywhere books are sold...

A painful break-up/break-down chases high-tech marketing wiz Sandy Lowiltry from her Silicon Valley home. She comes to rest  on the Oregon Coast, where she seeks solace in the opera-themed sanctuary of the Hotel Bel Canto and the arms of a handsome eccentric who spends his days combing the beach for sea glass.

Sandy soon learns what the tourist ladies already know — it's easy to fall for Frosted Glass Man. Besides great sex and alarmingly intricate campsite cuisine, Frosty offers do-it-yourself mythologies that would melt even the coldest heart. But will it be enough to quiet the whisper of ambition, the voice inside Sandy's head that chides her for settling? Will she really leave behind Silicon Valley for love in such a strange package?

"…a most unlikely tale of discovery and passion. …a shimmering fable, as delicate and whimsical as a handful of glass."
   – Debra Bokur, *Many Mountains Moving* literary journal

"A breezy, richly-textured romp through the inner circuitry of a postmodern heroine."
   – Christina Waters, PhD, *Metro* Newspapers (San Jose)

…available everywhere books are sold…

Gabriella's VOICE
THE NOVEL

Michael J. Vaughn

Fifty-year-old Bill Harness is on a strange but seemingly benign journey, rambling across the country in an old Pontiac and anonymously leaving large checks with promising young opera singers. His fuel, however, is sorrow, and it isn't until he arrives on a small island outside of Seattle and befriends Gabriella Compton, a phenomenally talented soprano, that he is able to address the three great tragedies of his vocally gifted family.

chael J. Vaughn has turned out a beautiful, lyrical novel. I was caught up e narrative within three sentences and was held spellbound by the story the end. It is as captivating as a well-performed *La Boheme*, as tragic triumphant as *Tosca*."

– Ani Harrison, *Tacoma Reporter*

turns rousing, lyrical and intoxicating, GABRIELLA'S VOICE is the of a virtuoso."

– Calder Lowe, *The Montserrat Review*

ighn performs the… task of invoking sounds from the silence of words on r. Arias whirl from the pages… a treat for the ear as well as the mind."

– Gregory Harris, *BookPage*

…available everywhere books are sold…

Also available in screenplay format!

Dead End Street® also highly recommends this title:

Suzanne Rosewell is the youngest female partner in the history of her prestigious Wall Street law firm. She's a strong, driven woman with the will to succeed. Then she meets Elias Garner, an enigmatic black Jazz musician who carries an ancient golden trumpet and represents the even more furtive "Chairman" (whom we learn heads the most powerful corporation on earth).

Elias explains that God has always placed among us thirty-six righteous people – each of whom "knows the divine will" and all of which must be accounted for if humanity is to redeem itself. Five are missing from the Chairman's list and Suzanne is asked to set aside her career to search for them. If she is unsuccessful, it appears that the world cannot exist beyond the sunrise.

...available everywhere books are sold...

ANOTHER FINE OFFERING FROM

DEAD END STREET®

www.ingramcontent.com/pod-product-compliance
Lightning Source LLC
Chambersburg PA
CBHW050747250626
47155CB00005B/1966